THE
TENTH
HOLIDAY
BOOK

THE TENTH
HOLIDAY BOOK

by

Enid Blyton

LONDON
SAMPSON LOW, MARSTON & CO. LTD.
AND D.V. PUBLICATIONS, LTD.

Made and Printed in Great Britain by Purnell & Sons, Ltd.
Paulton (Somerset) and London

This book may only be exported for sale in the following territories
by the appointed sole agents: AUSTRALIA—Ponsford, Newman
& Benson, Ltd. NEW ZEALAND—Whitcombe & Tombs, Ltd.
SOUTH AFRICA—Purnell & Sons (S.A.) (Pty), Ltd.

Contents

CONTENTS

Dust Wrapper designed by
HILDA BOSWELL

Endpapers by
CICELY STEED

Colour Plates by
CEDRIC CHATER

NOBODY LIKED HIM

"Look—there's Mr. Ugly!" said Joan, and she nudged Fred. "Is that his real name?" said Fred, surprised. "It does suit him, doesn't it?"

It wasn't his real name, of course, but it certainly suited the poor old man who was coming shuffling down the street. He had a very big nose, enormous shaggy eyebrows, eyes set so deep that you could hardly see them, and across one of his cheeks ran a long ugly scar that gave him a most peculiar look.

"I don't like him," said Fred. "Let's cross over to the other side of the road."

"Nobody likes him—except perhaps Madame Romano, his sister," said Joan, as they hurriedly crossed to the other side of the road. "She looks after him, and Mother says she's very kind to him. I don't like her, either—she's much too fat and she wears a wig."

"Does she really?" said Fred. "What a queer pair! I really don't like old Mr. Ugly—he looks as if he hasn't got any eyes at all, they're sunk so deep!"

None of the children liked old Mr. Ugly. Some of them were horrid to him. They called names after him, and once a boy called Daniel threw a stone at him. But the others soon stopped that. They knew that throwing stones was a cowardly thing to do.

Mr. Ugly had a very fierce temper. Once when Tom and Pat ran into him round a corner he caught hold of them and shook them just like a dog

John didn't wait to hear any more.
He darted off, scared.

shakes a rat! They were very frightened, especially as Mr. Ugly shouted all kinds of things in a language they didn't understand.

"It sounded as if he was yelling magic spells at us, or something!" said Pat afterwards. "Horrid old man! I hate him!"

Another time Mr. Ugly stopped little John on his way to school and asked him if he knew where a certain street was.

John was polite, and although he was half frightened of Mr. Ugly he spoke up well.

"Yes, Mr. Ugly, I know where the street is—you go down there and turn . . ."

Now he didn't mean to call the old man by his nickname Mr. Ugly, of course—he just didn't think. All the children used the name when they spoke of the old man, and some of them half thought that he had no other name. But how angry the old man was when he heard John call him Mr. Ugly!

He made a grab at him, and John just dodged in time. "Bad boy! Impolite boy! That is not my name. Ah, you children of nowadays are not like the children I once knew—how they came to me then, and how they laughed and said, 'Again, dear Uncle Koffti, again!' But you, you are horrid children; you are unkind and cruel to a poor old man. I tell you, ugly manners are worse than an ugly face! I tell you . . ."

But John didn't wait to hear any more. He darted off, scared, wondering if the old fellow was mad. What did he mean, talking about children of other days, calling himself Uncle Koffti? . . . Yes, he must be mad!

The other children laughed when John told them about all this. But his mother didn't laugh.

"John, he is almost blind and very lame," she said. "However ugly and queer he is, remember that he can hardly see anything, and can only walk very, very slowly. You are lucky—you can run faster than anyone at school, and you have eyes so sharp that you can see the highest lark in the sky."

John said no more. Mother was kind, and she was always right about things—but surely she didn't quite understand how frightening old Mr. Ugly was, with his shaggy eyebrows and his half-hidden eyes—and that queer scar across his cheek.

Now, that term all the children in the school were making presents for poor children who had no toys, or for the children in the hospital. Joan had made a rag doll that could be cuddled and felt very cosy and comfortable. Fred had made a scrap-book filled with the very nicest pictures he could find to cut out. John had made a soft woolly ball, and so had Doris. It was fun to look in the cupboard and see all the things collecting there, one by one.

That term all the children in the school were making presents for poor children who had no toys, or for the children in the hospital.

13

But when the stick was finished Lame Lennie had gone away! "Well, now—who can we give it to?" wondered Miss Brown.

"I'd like to make something for a grown-up now," said John when he had finished his ball. "Can I make something for old Kate, who cleans our school for us, Miss Brown? Do let me."

"Yes. That would be very nice," said Miss Brown, pleased. " But what will you make her?"

"I could make her a photograph frame and put a picture of all of us into it—the school photo we had this year," said John. "I know Kate would like that."

"Can I make something for a grown-up, too?" said Peter. "My father has cut some sticks from the hazel hedge, and he says he can show me how to carve the head of one and then varnish and polish the stick so that it looks like a really proper one."

"That would be a fine idea," said Miss Brown. "We'll give it to Lame Lennie, shall we?"

Lame Lennie was the gardener, and he was very nice indeed. He had lost a leg in the war, and, although he had a wooden one instead, he liked to walk with a stick

"Yes—I'll give it to Lame Lennie," said Peter.

But when the stick was finished Lame Lennie had gone away! His good leg had got something wrong with it and he was sent right away to hospital. So the stick couldn't be given to him.

"Well, now—whom can we give it to?" wondered Miss Brown. "Let's think hard."

But nobody could think of anyone to give the stick to at all. And then Miss Brown had an idea.

"I know! We'll send it to that poor old man who lives with his sister at the end of the village—I can't remember his name."

"Mr. Ugly, do you mean?" asked Joan.

"I know you call him that," said Miss Brown. "Poor old fellow! Yes, that's the man I mean. I meet him shuffling along sometimes, and I feel sorry for him. He would be so pleased to have an unexpected present like this. Don't you think so, children?"

There was no answer at all. The children looked at one another. Fancy giving a present—and such a nice one, too—to old Mr. Ugly, that bad-tempered, horrid old man! Why, Miss Brown was really quite stupid!

The teacher was surprised to get no answer. She tapped on her desk. "I'm asking you a question, children! Don't you think it would please the old man to have such a nice, unexpected present?"

"It might please him—but it wouldn't please *us* to give it to him," said Peter. "I didn't make such a nice stick to give away to somebody horrid."

Miss Brown looked shocked. "Peter! Surely you can spare a bit of kindness to a poor, half-blind old fellow even if you *do* think he's horrid!"

"All right, Miss Brown," said Peter, going red. "But—*I'm* not going to give it to him. Somebody else can!"

"I shan't! I shan't!" called the rest of the children at once.

"It might please him, but it wouldn't please *us* to give it to him," said Peter.

"The one whose name is drawn out will go to give the stick—and let me have no more nonsense about this, please!"

Miss Brown looked vexed.

"Very well. We will draw for it. I will put all your names into a tin and Joan shall draw out one of them. The one whose name is drawn out will go to give the stick—and let me have no more nonsense about this, please!"

She put the names into a tin. Joan was told to go and draw one out. She picked out a bit of paper and unfolded it.

"Jennifer!" she said. "It's you, Jennifer."

Oh dear! Jennifer stared at Miss Brown in alarm. She was a quiet little mouse of a girl, and she couldn't bear to think she must go to Mr. Ugly's house and knock at the door. Suppose he answered it himself and shouted at her?

"I can't, I can't," said Jennifer.

"Don't be so silly," said Miss Brown, getting cross. "All this fuss and bother over a simple little thing! I'm glad it's you, Jennifer. It's time you stopped being such a little mouse and had to *do* something!"

Jennifer took the stick at the end of afternoon school. It had a label tied to the top of it. "This stick comes with best wishes from the school-children. It was made by Peter Biggs." Jennifer didn't go to Mr. Ugly's cottage straight away. She went home first. She meant to get Josie, her doll. She wouldn't feel quite so scared if she had Josie with her. Josie never looked afraid of anything. She had a bold, bright, smiling face, and Jennifer loved her very much.

She set off with the stick in one hand and Josie under the other arm. She came to the little cottage where old Mr. Ugly lived with Madame Romano, his sister. The little garden was gay with snowdrops. Jennifer had never seen so many! She walked nervously up the little path and knocked on the door. Mr. Ugly opened it.

Jennifer suddenly lost her tongue. She held the stick out to him, but he didn't take it.

"What do you want? Can't you speak, child?" he said.

"It's—it's——" began poor Jennifer, and couldn't say another word.

"Bah!" said the old man in a most terrifying manner. Jennifer couldn't stay a minute longer. She pushed the stick into Mr. Ugly's hand and fled down the path. But, alas, she caught her foot on a stone and fell over on her face. She wasn't hurt, and picked herself up at once—and then she gave such a heart-rending cry that Mr. Ugly almost jumped out of his skin.

Jennifer suddenly lost her tongue. She held the stick out to him,
but he didn't take it.

17

"Ossie! This little girl brought
a present for you, see?"

"Oh, Josie, you're broken! Your poor face—it's cracked in half!"

Jennifer sat down on the path and nursed her broken doll, so unhappy that she forgot all about Mr. Ugly. But the old man came hurrying out, and behind him came his plump old sister.

"What is it, my little one, what is it?" said Madame Romano. "You have hurt yourself, yes? And oh, your poor, poor doll! See, Ossie, her doll is broken!"

"Ah, the poor darling!" said Mr. Ugly, and he peered down at the doll. He took it gently out of Jennifer's arm. Madame Romano picked up the stick, which had been dropped on the path. She read the label and gave a cry of delight.

"Ossie! This little girl brought a present for you, see? A beautiful stick, oh, a wonder-stick, this is! For you, Ossie, for you. And you thought the children all hated you, my poor old ugly brother! Why, they have made this wonder-stick for *you*!"

"For me?" said her brother. "And this kind little girl came to give it to me—but she was frightened of me. And now her doll is broken. Greta, we must take her in and comfort her. We must show her *our* dolls!"

Jennifer was led indoors, still crying. And then she had a great surprise. She went into a tiny room with shelves all round it, and sitting on the shelves were dolls of all kinds and sizes—lovely dolls with carved wooden faces and with jointed arms and legs, ankles and wrists, all dressed in quaint and beautiful dresses. Jennifer stared round in astonishment.

"But—what are they?" she said "They are not like ordinary dolls."

"No, no, little one—they are puppet-dolls," said Mr. Ugly, and he took one down. Then Jennifer saw that it had strings attached to its arms and legs and head. "See, this is little Melisande—how she dances, this little Melisande!"

And, indeed, how the little puppet-doll danced when Mr. Ugly held her up by her strings, pulling this one and that to make the puppet dance and fling her arms about as if she was really alive!

"But—really she seems a live doll," said Jennifer in wonder. "Oh, I love her. Do the others dance, too?"

"Yes, they all dance—and they act, too," said Madame Romano, making a sailor doll do the hornpipe. "See him kick! Ah, he is a clever one, this doll."

"Where did you get them all?" asked Jennifer.

"We made them," said Mr. Ugly. "I made the dolls and my sister made the dresses. We lived in Austria, and we went round with our dolls and

How the little doll danced when Mr. Ugly held her up by her strings, pulling this one and that to make the puppet dance.

"Oh, Mr. Ugly, could you bring some of your dolls one afternoon and
show them to the whole school?"

made them dance to amuse the little children. Then, alas, war came, and
we do not want to live anywhere but here. Now I am nearly blind, and I
am old and ugly and nobody wants me, or my dolls. And yet they can
dance so beautifully! But you children—you do not like such things."

"Please," said Jennifer, taking the old man's hand, "we didn't know
anything about you. But oh, if only you would let us come and see your
dolls—if you would make them dance and act for us—we would like them
just as much as the Austrian children did. More."

"Ah—but would you like me, too?" said Mr. Ugly, and he shook his
head. "Nobody likes me any more—except Greta, my sister."

Jennifer looked at him. He didn't look ugly any more. He looked
kind and sad and gentle.

"*I* like you," she said. "And the others would, too. Oh, Mr. Ugly,
could you bring some of your dolls one afternoon and show them to the
whole school? Miss Brown would love that. Oh, do, do! "

"Now, Ossie—what fun that would be!" said his sister. "Yes, my
little one, I will make him do that. He loves children, and he and his dolls
should be with them. You tell your teacher we will come when she says.
And see, here is a doll for you instead of your poor broken one. You
shall show it to the children, and tell them soon we will come with others."

Jennifer looked down at the pretty little puppet-doll.

20

"Her name is Gretchen," said Madame Romano. "She is yours. And you shall take a big bunch of snowdrops for your kind teacher," said the kind old woman, hurrying into the garden, where she picked about a hundred snowdrops! "Ah, it is good to see a kind little girl like you."

"Oh, thank you," said Jennifer. " Miss Brown *will* be pleased. I'll tell her you and—and—Mr. Ugly will come. Oh dear—I mustn't call him Mr. Ugly. What's his real name?"

"You can call me Uncle Koffti," said the old man. "If you like me and are my friend you can call me what all the other children have called me—your Uncle Koffti!"

Miss Brown and the children could hardly believe Jennifer's tale next day, but they had to when she showed them the snowdrops and the lovely little puppet Gretchen. Miss Brown beamed round the class.

"We'll ask the kind old fellow and his sister to come next Wednesday afternoon—and we'll have a tea-party, shall we, and ask them to that, too! We *shall* have fun!"

"Miss Brown, I'm so glad you made us give the stick to Mr. Ugly," said Peter. "It's made him happy—and he's going to make us happy!"

He certainly is. If only I could be there on Wednesday afternoon and see Uncle Koffti make all his puppets dance and curtsey! It's really wonderful what a little bit of kindness will do, isn't it?

Miss Brown and the children could hardly believe Jennifer's tale next day, but they had to when she showed them the snowdrops.

THE WISH THAT CAME TRUE

PIPPY and Flip were flying their big kite. It pulled at its string as hard as it could.

"It's a fine kite," said Pippy. "It flies well."

"It will bump into that cloud if it doesn't look out," said Flip. "There —it has, and it's taken a little corner out of it, too."

"Let me hold it for a bit," said Pippy. So he held it and enjoyed feeling the tug and pull of the eager kite far away up in the sky.

"Pippy! Flip!" called their mother. "It's dinner-time. Come along quickly. Haul down your kite and put it away."

"Oh no, Ma!" called Pippy. "It's flying so well. Can't we tie it up and leave it to fly?"

"No," said his mother. "Pull it down. You know we're going over to old Dame See-Saw after dinner, and we'll have to run to catch the bus, I expect. Pull your kite down at once."

"Don't let's," whispered Pippy. "Let's tie it to something and it can fly all the time we're having dinner. It will love that."

"What can we tie it to?" asked Flip. "Oooh, I know—let's tie it to Ma's old garden chair. That will hold it well."

So they tied it to their mother's old garden chair and then went in to their dinner. But whilst they were having their dinner, the wind grew very much stronger. It was almost a gale. Whoooooooooo-hoooo-hooo, it went, and the kite tugged hard at its string. The old garden chair gave a sudden little hop. The kite had pulled so hard

22

that it made it move. The kite tugged at its string again and the chair gave another little hop.

Then the wind blew so hard that the kite tugged wildly—and will you believe it, up into the air went the old garden chair, swinging at the end of the long, long string!

The kite flew higher in the sky and farther away. The chair hopped over the wall and flew up into the air, too, and it even flew over the roof of a cottage. My word, it was having the time of its life!

It flew and it flew, and then—dear me, the knot in the string began to come loose! Soon the chair would fall. It might break itself into pieces. It began to be afraid.

The wind dropped a little, and the kite flew lower. The chair dropped lower, too, and almost touched a wall it was swinging over. Suddenly the knot came undone, and the string parted from the back of the chair.

But it hadn't really very far to fall. It fell into a little garden, behind a bush, and there it stood feeling shaky, wondering where it was.

Up into the air went the old garden chair, swinging at the end
of the long, long string!

"Bless us all—it's an old garden chair, dropped right out of the blue,
as I wished my wish!" she said.

Now old Dame See-Saw had been hanging out her washing on that lovely windy day. She had washed all the morning, and she was very, very tired. It was nice out in the garden, and she thought she would like a little rest out there.

"If only I had a garden chair to rest in and to ease my tired old legs, wouldn't that be lovely!" she thought, pegging up the last stocking. "How I wish I had a comfortable old garden chair for myself!"

Plop! Something fell down that very moment behind the nearby bush. Dame See-Saw was startled. She went to see what it was.

"Bless us all—it's an old garden chair, dropped right out of the blue, as I wished my wish!" she said in astonishment. "Well, there now—it's just what I want to sit in and rest my old legs. I'll have a little snooze."

So down she sat and shut her eyes. The chair was so comfortable and fitted her exactly. "It couldn't be better," she said sleepily. "Oh, how lovely to have a wish come true! I really must tell Pippy and Flip and their mother when they come to see me."

Well—they're on their way in the bus, of course. And what *do* you suppose Pippy's mother will think when she sees old Dame See-Saw fast asleep in the old garden chair that really belongs to *her*? And what will Pippy and Flip say?

Well, if ever a wish came true, Dame See-Saw's did that afternoon. And if I know anything about her, she's going to keep that chair!

As for the kite, it's still flying. Look out for it. It's black and blue, with a smiling face and a tail made of yellow and red. I'll let you know if I see it!

THE PARTY

You take off your coat and you
  change your shoes,
The party's begun, there's no
  time to lose,
You can hear them "Gathering
  Nuts in May",
And you're simply longing to go
  in and play.

There's Twirl-the-Tray, and you
  twirl it fast,
And Musical Chairs, and you're
  left in last,
There's Twos and Threes and
  General Post,
And you really don't know
  which you like the most.

There's tea, with ginger and
  chocolate cake,
And coloured jellies that shiver
  and shake,
There's trifle with cream, and
  pink strawberry ice,
There's Christmas cake, too, and
  they cut you a slice.

There are dozens of crackers to
  pull with a bang,
There's a Christmas tree, too, on
  which gay presents hang,
And then, oh dear, how the time
  does fly,
It's "Thank you for having me!"
  and "Goodbye!"

Mr. SMICK PLAYS A TRICK

"Now, LISTEN, Smick," said Mrs. Smick. "You're to be home in time for your dinner today. Monday you were late and the stew was spoiled. Tuesday you came in at half-past two, and the joint was . . ."

"Yes, dear; yes, dear," said Mr. Smick hastily. "You've told me all that before. I'll be in time today."

"You won't," said Mrs. Smick with a sigh. "You simply haven't any idea of time at all, Smick. And I gave you such a nice watch for Christmas, too."

"Well, don't I always wear it?" said Smick.

"Yes, but you hardly ever wind it," said Mrs. Smick, "so it never tells you the right time! And if it did you'd forget to look at it."

"I'll be in time today," promised Mr. Smick.

"You know your Aunt Melia is coming," said Mrs. Smick, "and your sister Mandy. I can't wait dinner for you. I know what you are when you get to market—you just wander round and poke your stick at the pigs, and rub the noses of the horses, and pull the sheep's wool—and you never once think of dinner sharp at one o'clock."

"I'd better be going," said Mr. Smick, who knew that his wife would rattle on like this for hours if he didn't go.

He took his stick and found his hat. Then just as he was going out Mrs. Smick called him. She had a sly smile on her face.

"Smick! Here, put the kitchen clock into your pocket. It's an alarm-clock, and I've set it for half-past twelve. It'll go off with a r-r-r-r-ring then, and you will know it's time to set off home. You'll be in time for dinner for once!"

"Oh dear!" said Smick, who really didn't want to carry alarm-clocks about with him. "All right. I'll put it in my pocket, and I daresay it will remind me to set off back home when it rings."

He put it into his pocket and walked down the garden path to the front gate. He found his small boy swinging on the gate.

"Hallo, Dad!" said Jiminy. "Going to market? I wish you'd bring me back a present. You forgot last time."

"So I did," said Mr. Smick. "Well, I really will remember this time. What do you want?"

"A toy telephone," said Jiminy. "Dad, could you get one?"

"But you can't really telephone with a *toy* telephone," said Mr. Smick. "It's a silly thing really. You can only talk into it, and never get a reply from anyone."

"I can pretend I'm talking to somebody who is talking back to me," said Jiminy. "That's all I need to do. Go on, Dad—buy me one if you can."

"Right," said Mr. Smick. "I will." Off he went, over the fields, up the hill, and through the wood to the market in the next town.

On the way he met Mr. Smack.

"Hallo, Smick," said Smack. "Just a word of warning. Those robbers are about again—you know, the three who set on old Mr. Sniff the other day and robbed him of his money. It's my belief they've got their hide-out somewhere in the wood."

"Dear me!" said Mr. Smick, alarmed. I'll be careful, then.

He found his small boy swinging on the gate. "Hallo, Dad!" said Jiminy.

I've got to go through the wood. I wish Mr. Plod, the policeman, would get hold of them. Nasty little creatures they are."

He went on, keeping a sharp look-out as he walked through the wood. But he saw and heard nobody. He came to the market and smiled with pleasure to sniff the good smell of animals, hear the bleatings and mooings and neighings. Ah, this was good! Plenty going on in the market!

He had a very happy time there, and then he suddenly remembered the toy telephone he had promised to take home to little Jiminy. He'd better get it at once.

He found a toyshop—and what a lucky thing, it had a toy telephone to sell. It was a dear little thing, with a piece to speak into, and a piece to listen to with your ear. It had a little stand and a long piece of black wire. Splendid! Jiminy would love that.

"I'll buy this," said Mr. Smick, and put his hand in his pocket to get his money. He touched something round and hard. Whatever could it be?

Then he remembered. Of course—it was the kitchen clock that Mrs. Smick had popped into his pocket. She had set the alarm to go off at half-past twelve.

Mr. Smick looked hastily at the clock in the toyshop. He sighed with relief. It was only ten-past twelve. That tiresome clock wouldn't start ringing yet.

He got to the market and smiled with pleasure to sniff the good smell of animals,
and hear the bleatings and mooings.

He made up his mind to set off home before it did. His friends in the market would laugh at him if they heard the alarm-clock ringing in his pocket. So after he had paid for the telephone and tucked it under his arm he walked through the market and set off on his way home.

He came to the wood. He remembered what Mr. Smack had told him about the robbers. Oh dear! The sun had gone in, the sky was black with clouds, and it seemed very dark indeed under the trees.

"Robbers might be waiting for me anywhere," thought Mr. Smick nervously.

Then he heard the blackbird singing loudly nearby.

"Anyway, they shan't get Jiminy's little telephone," he thought.

"Smick, Smick, Smick! Mind how you go, mind how you go! R-r-r-r-r-r-robbers are near, near, near. R-r-r-r-robbers! Smick, Smick, Smick!"

Smick was most alarmed. Robbers! They would set on him and rob him. He had a lot of money in his pockets, too.

He heard whispering nearby. He felt sure he could see the top of a stick, and the point of somebody's hat behind a bush. He stopped in fright.

"Anyway, they shan't get Jiminy's little telephone," he thought, and he put it up into the tree nearby. And just at that very moment out leapt the three nasty robbers with yells and shouts. They were goblins, and they had sticks that they flourished in a very horrid way.

"Give us your money!" they cried, and they ran at Mr. Smick.

It was exactly half-past twelve. The kitchen clock in Mr. Smick's pocket went off at once, and the alarm rang loudly.

"R-r-r-r-r-ring! R-r-r-r-r-ring! R-r-r-r-r-ring!"

29.

And, indeed, the alarm-clock did sound exactly like a telephone ringing.
"R-r-r-r-r-ring! R-r-r-r-r-ring!"

The three robbers stopped in astonishment. They had no idea that Mr. Smick had an alarm-clock in his pocket, of course.

"A telephone ringing!" said one robber.

"Here in the woods!" cried another.

"What an extraordinary thing!" said the third.

And, indeed, the alarm-clock did sound exactly like a telephone ringing. "R-r-r-r-r-ring! R-r-r-r-r-ring!"

Then Mr. Smick had an idea, the best he had ever had in his life.

"Pardon me," he said politely to the surprised robbers. "That's the telephone ringing. Permit me to answer it before you rob me."

"Yes. Yes, certainly," said the biggest goblin, anxious to see where this mysterious telephone was.

Mr. Smick reached up to the tree where he had put the toy telephone. He took down the receiver and put it to his mouth and ear.

"Hallo!" he said, just as if he were Jiminy having a pretend talk to somebody. "HALLO! I can't quite hear you. Who is it?"

He paused as if he were listening to someone at the other end. The three robbers gaped at him. A telephone up a tree in the middle of the woods! Whoever heard of such a thing? How truly remarkable!

"Oh—it's you—Mr. Plod, the policeman," said Mr. Smick. "Good morning, Smick here—Mr. Tobias Smick. What can I do for you?"

The three robbers backed away a little. Good gracious! Could that really be their enemy, Mr. Plod, the policeman, on the telephone?

"Yes, Mr. Plod. Three robbers, did you say? They've just set on me—nasty little creatures they are. You want them caught, do you? Well, I'll tell you exactly where I am in the wood, and you can send three men here to get them. Or, better still, surround the wood. What, you are coming along yourself, too, Mr. Plod? Oh, fine, fine!"

The robbers turned pale. They looked at one another. Mr. Plod was coming! He was sending men to catch them! The wood might be surrounded!

"Yes, Mr. Plod," said Mr. Smick, "I'll stay here with them till you come. They want to rob me, so that will take a little time—and by then you should have been able to surround the wood. You can't imagine what nasty, ugly little things they are."

Mr. Smick was enjoying himself tremendously. He had no idea that it was such fun to pretend like this. No wonder Jiminy liked it! He glanced round to see whether the robbers were trembling and shivering.

"Oh—it's you—Mr. Plod, the policeman," said Mr. Smick. "Good morning."

31

There was nobody there! One by one the bad little creatures had slipped away between the bushes, afraid of seeing Mr. Plod arriving at any minute! Mr. Smick was alone.

He gave a sigh of relief. He popped the toy telephone under his coat and set off home, grinning whenever he thought of his pretend telephone call. Dear, dear, how he had enjoyed that!

He got home punctually at one, and Mrs. Smick was very pleased with him. "Good!" she said. "The alarm-clock was a very good idea, Smick. Your aunt and sister are in the garden, tell them dinner is ready."

"The alarm-clock was a much better idea than you knew, wife," said Mr. Smick. "Where's Jiminy? I've got a toy telephone for him—and a wonderful story to tell, as well!"

The three goblins never robbed anyone again. They were so afraid of telephones ringing in the wood! They went back to the tree in which Smick had put the toy telephone—but they never found it, of course.

And that wasn't surprising, because it's in Jiminy's playroom, and you'd be surprised at the telephone calls he makes every day. He rings up all kinds of people and talks away to them—he spoke to the Queen the other day, and to the President of the United States. He'll probably ring me up, too, if he thinks of it.

He'd get a surprise if I answered, wouldn't he!

He got home punctually at one, and Mrs. Smick was very pleased with him. "Good!" she said. "The alarm-clock was a very good idea."

Adventure for two

"COMING with me in the car?" called Daddy to Jack and Mary. "I'm just going down to see old Mrs. Blakey."

"Oh, is she ill?" said Mary. Her daddy was a doctor and went to see ill people every day.

"No, not ill. She's sprained her ankle, that's all," said Daddy. " I'm just going to have a look at it—and then I rather thought I'd go to the bakery and have one of those chocolate ice-creams of theirs. But you know how I hate eating ice-creams alone."

"Oooh, Daddy! Of course we'll come!" said Jack. He came running out of the playroom with Mary. "You're a brick, Daddy! You always tell us when you're going ice-creaming!"

They went to get their hats and coats. Their father went out to get his car. He brought it into the front drive.

Jack and Mary came running out. "I'll go in the front now, and you can be there coming back," said Mary to Jack. In they got, and off went the car. Down the drive, out into the road, and up the hill. Down the hill and round the corner—and there was old Mrs. Blakey's house, with its thick yew hedge all round the front garden.

"Now you just look after my car for me whilst I'm in the house," said Daddy, "then I shan't need to lock it up. I always have to if there's nobody in it, because my precious case of medicines might be stolen."

"Oh, yes," said Jack. "And some of them are very poisonous, aren't they?"

Daddy went up the path to the house. The children sat in the car, looking at the thick yew hedge. Mary got out.

"I just want to look at the hedge," she said to Jack. "It's so very, very thick. Why, it's thick enough to get right into the middle of it!"

Jack got out, too. They had always liked old Mrs. Blakey's thick yew hedge. Mary parted the green boughs and looked into the depths of the dark hedge.

"Jack!" she said. "Look! There's a kind of passage going right along the middle of the hedge!"

Jack looked. It did really seem like a passage! The leaves there had dried and fallen off, and the middle of the hedge was empty and bare.

"We could almost go along it," said Jack. "Mary—shall we just get into it for a minute? I believe if we were in the very middle nobody could possibly see us! What a wonderful hiding-place it would make!"

"Let's hide from Daddy!" said Mary at once. "That *would* be fun! He'd come out and look for us—and we wouldn't be there!"

Jack looked. It did really seem like a passage! The leaves there had dried
and fallen off, and the middle of the hedge was empty.

"And we could say something in a very deep, hollow kind of voice," said Jack. "It would make him jump! Come on, Mary, before he comes out."

It was easy to squeeze into the thick yew hedge. Once in the centre the branches closed firmly round them, and nobody could see them.

"But I've got a fine peep-hole, Mary—have you?" asked Jack. "I can see Daddy's car through it."

"Yes. I've got a peep-hole, too—between some leaves," said Mary. "Jack—supposing somebody comes by—had we better keep still and quiet?"

"Yes," said Jack. "We can't give our hiding-place away!"

"Now there's a woman coming," whispered Jack. The woman passed, walking quickly.

"I can hear someone coming now," said Mary, and she looked through her peep-hole. "It's Jimmy White!"

Jimmy passed by, whistling cheerfully. Jack and Mary giggled. They longed to say "Beware, Jimmy!" in a deep, peculiar voice, but they knew Jimmy well enough to know that he would at once go to look in the hedge for the voice!

"Now there's a woman coming," whispered Jack. "I don't know her."

The woman passed, walking quickly. The children sat quite still in their hiding-place. The passer-by didn't know anyone was so near her!

Nobody came for a little while. Then Jack heard soft footsteps. He peeped out.

"Two men, Mary," he whispered. "Aren't they walking quietly!"

The men came up to the car—but they didn't walk past. They stopped just by it. The children held their breath in case their hiding-place should be discovered.

He wrenched the front door of the car open and put his hand in quickly. In a
trice he had taken the case and had shut the door quietly.

"No one about," said one man in a very low voice. "Whose car's
this? It's got a case inside."

"It's Doctor Fenton's car," said the other man in such a low voice
that the children could hardly hear him. "That will be his case.
There will be valuable drugs in there. Any chance of getting them?"

"Better try now, whilst there's no one to see," said the first man. He
wrenched the front door of the car open and put his hand in quickly. In
a trice he had taken the case and had shut the door quietly.

Then the two men moved off quickly, walking very softly.

The children had seen all this, and were absolutely thunderstruck.
Two robbers! Thieves who had dared to open their father's car and take
his case—in full daylight, too! Well, you read of such things in the
newspapers—but they never, never happened under your nose like this!

"Mary!" said Jack, finding his tongue at last. "We didn't do a thing.
We never even shouted."

"I couldn't," said Mary. "It all happened so quickly. What are we
going to do? Daddy's case is gone."

"And we were supposed to be in charge of it," said Jack, horrified at
the thought. "Goodness—we were pretty feeble, Mary. If only we'd just
given one shout those men would have shot off at once, without even
opening the car."

"Yes, but it all happened so *quickly*," said Mary, almost in tears. "I couldn't say a word. I did try, but I couldn't. Let's get out of this hedge and tell Daddy."

At that very moment they heard the front door slam, and their father came briskly down the path. "Now what about our ice-creams?" he called, as he got to the gate.

Jack and Mary were just climbing out of the hedge. They looked un-tidy and were covered with little bits and pieces. They looked so very solemn that their father was surprised.

"I say—did you *have* to climb into that dirty old hedge?" he said, opening his car. Then he stopped and stared. "Good gracious—where's my case gone?"

"Daddy, it's been stolen," said Jack. "Oh, Daddy, it was our fault. We were in the hedge when the men came by and we . . ."

"Now begin at the beginning and tell me everything," said Daddy, seeing at once that something serious had happened. So the children told him everything: how they had got into the hedge, how people had come by, and the two men had come and talked, and then had stolen the case.

"Did they see you?" asked Daddy. "Did they know you were there?"

"Oh no," said Jack. "But we saw *them* all right. We know exactly what they are like and how they are dressed. If we saw them again we'd know them."

They looked untidy and were covered with little bits and pieces.

37

He went first to the police-station, and was given an extra passenger—a burly
policeman dressed in ordinary clothes.

"Very well, then—hop quickly into the car," said Daddy. "I'll go to
the police-station and collect a policeman in plain clothes, and we'll drive
slowly round and about the streets. Maybe we'll see those men again!"

This was all very exciting indeed. The children got into the car, and
Daddy drove off. He went first to the police-station, told very shortly
what had happened, and was given an extra passenger—a burly policeman
dressed in ordinary clothes.

"They'll have wrapped up that case of yours in brown paper now, sir,"
said the policeman. "No good looking for the case—have to look for a
large brown-paper parcel, or a suitcase big enough to have put your case in.
They wouldn't be foolish enough to carry your bag openly for long. Good
thing these youngsters of yours noticed what the men were like!"

The car drove slowly down one street and up another. "There are two
men," said the policeman suddenly. "Sitting on that seat, sir; look—with
a big parcel."

"No—that's not the men," said Jack. "Is it, Mary? Our men had
different clothes—one was in a brown suit with a brown tie, and the other
was in a green coat with a black tie."

"Right. Go on again, sir, please," said the policeman. "Ah, wait—
what about these men coming round the corner with a case?"

The men had on the right-coloured suits, but they were not a bit like
the ones the children had seen.

"No—both those men are small," said Mary, "and our men are tall.
One had a little moustache and the other hadn't. And they both wore hats
like Daddy's, and one man had a tiny feather stuck into his hat-band."

"My word—these kids of yours notice a lot, don't they?" said the policeman, most impressed. "They'll be telling us how many toes the men had next!"

The children laughed. They were keeping a very close look-out indeed. They had felt so ashamed of letting those men steal their father's case under their very noses; now they felt they really must catch them and get the case back, or they would never forgive themselves.

Up the hill and down. No men at all. Round the town and back again. Plenty of men, but not the ones they wanted.

"Of course they might have gone into a shop somewhere, or the cinema," said the policeman. "They've had time to get a good way away now, and unless they caught a bus or a train they'll probably be sitting down having tea somewhere—or seeing a film. I'm afraid we'll have to give up finding them this way, sir. I've got all particulars from the children—though I'd like to ask them a few questions—and we'll send out descriptions of the men everywhere."

Up the hill and down. No men at all. Round the town and back again.
Plenty of men, but not the ones they wanted.

"Right," said Dr. Fenton. "Well, would you like to come along to my house and ask the children what else you want to know?"

Mary spoke up in a very small voice:

"Daddy, I suppose we don't deserve those ice-creams now, do we?"

"Bless us all!" said Daddy. "I'd quite forgotten we were going to have some. Yes, of course we'll have them. Constable, will you join us? You can ask your questions in the bakery."

"Yes, sir. It would be quite a treat," said the policeman, beaming round at the two children. "It's a long time since I was taken out to have an ice-cream."

They came to the bakery, and they got out. This time Daddy locked his car well and truly. "Though it's rather like locking the stable door after the horse has gone," he told the children. "Come along."

They went into the tea-room of the bakery, but it was tea-time now and the place was full. "I've a little room upstairs," said the shop-woman. "I think there's a table up there, sir."

So up they went and found the table. A girl came to take their order. Whilst they were waiting for their ice-creams the two children looked round the room. They had never been in this little room before, and they didn't think it was as nice as the big one downstairs. Still, the ice-creams would be just as good!

Mary suddenly trod hard on Jack's toe. Jack looked at her in surprise. Then he looked where she was looking, and he went bright red with excitement.

Then Jack looked where she was looking, and he went bright red with excitement.

Under the table was a very large suitcase! Both children felt certain
their father's smaller case was inside it.

Sitting huddled together in the darkest corner of the little room were
the two men who had stolen their father's case! There was no mistaking
them at all—one with a little moustache, one with none; one with a green
coat and black tie, and the other in brown with a brown tie.

And under the table was a very large suitcase! They looked at one
another. They didn't dare to whisper their news in case the men sus-
pected something. So Jack took out his little notebook and pencil and
scribbled something in it. He passed it silently to his father.

"*Those are the men over there. Look at the suitcase under the table!*" That
was what he had written.

His father passed the note to the policeman, who lighted a cigarette
and looked casually over at the two men as he did so. He in turn scribbled
a note very quickly and had it ready for the girl when she came with their
ice-creams. His note was short and clear.

"*Take this to the police-station,*" was written on the outside. And inside: "*Send two men to Harrison's Bakery at once. Upstairs. Johns.*"

The girl brought their ice-creams, took the note, looked at the outside, seemed very scared, and went out quietly. Two other people finished
their tea and went. That left only the two men and the children's table.

The girl came back and slid a note into the policeman's hands. One of
the two men called out to her.

"Hey, miss—what time does the bus to Highlands go?"

"Not for fifteen minutes, sir," said the girl.

"Good," thought the children. "The men won't slip out yet."

Two strange men came into the tea-room and sat down silently at the table next to the children's. They nodded to the policeman, who at once got up and went over to the two men.

"I have reason to think that there is stolen property in that bag of yours," he said. "Will you open it?"

The men leapt up at once, blustering angrily. One caught up the case. "What cheek!" he said. "Who are you to say things like that! I'll report you to the police."

"I *am* the police," said the policeman stolidly. "Open that bag, please."

The men pushed him aside and went to the door. But the other two policemen were there now. No escape that way!

"Huh! Three of you!" said one of the men in disgust. "All right. Open the case. Though how you know it was us that did the job I don't know. There wasn't anyone to see."

"Walls have ears," said the policeman, opening the bag and taking out Doctor Fenton's bag from inside. "And hedges have eyes!"

Well, of course, the two men had no idea what he was talking about, but the children knew! They were pleased to see the two men marched off.

"I'm glad you've got your bag back, Daddy," said Mary. "We were silly to let it be stolen. What a good thing we came here for ice-creams!"

"It was," said Daddy. "I say—what about another one each just to celebrate your exciting adventure!"

CAN YOU DO THIS CROSSWORD PUZZLE?

ACROSS

At night upon my first you look,
My second's owned by everyone,
My third you do to door or book,
The meaning of my fourth is gone.

DOWN

My first is very soft and light,
My second may be used for string,
You say my third in prayer each night,
My fourth's a tear in anything.

Answer on page 174.

43

THE TIRESOME SAILOR DOLL

"Sailor doll is so *tiresome*," said the golden-haired doll. "He does such silly things."

"Yes. He tied the clockwork mouse's tail to a bootlace yesterday when he was asleep," said the teddy-bear. "And when the mouse woke up Sailor told him a snake was eating his tail up, and he ran for miles round the nursery, with his bootlace tail behind him. He really did think it was a snake."

"And Sailor wetted me through," said the black toy dog. "He got the little watering-can and filled it. Then he climbed up on the table and watered me when I sat underneath. I thought it was raining."

"And he burst a paper bag near me and told me the captain of the soldiers had shot at me," said the golliwog. "I felt awfully frightened. I thought I was wounded and I looked all over me to see."

"And now he's discovered that money-box up on the shelf," said the teddy-bear. "It's just like a letter-box—you know, it's got a slit to put pennies in—and Sailor keeps posting things in it."

" He's posted my best handkerchief," said Angela, the doll.

"And he tried to post my best brooch yesterday. I just stopped him in time," said the baby doll.

"He'll post the clockwork mouse's key if he's not careful," said the golliwog. The mouse gave a squeal of terror.

"It's all right. If Sailor does that we'll punish him," said the golden-haired doll in a loud voice.

Sailor didn't care! If he was in a naughty mood he'd do anything. Why, he had once climbed up to the wash-basin, put in the plug, and turned on a tap! The toys were very frightened when the water overflowed all over the carpet.

"Get into the ark, get into Noah's ark, there are floods coming!" the naughty sailor doll had shouted.

So you see, he really would do anything; and when he heard the toys talking about him he felt naughtier than ever.

He took one of the baby doll's shoes and posted that in the money-box. He took the little necklace belonging to Angela, broke it, and posted the beads one by one. Clinkity-clinkity-clink they went, and dropped down among the pennies and ha'pennies in the box.

He even took the tiny plates out of the dolls'-house and posted those in the money-box, too. The dolls were very angry indeed.

"That's too bad of you, Sailor!" they cried. "Now we can't give our party. You've posted the plates."

"What do I care?" said Sailor. "You wouldn't have asked me to your party, anyhow. I don't mind that, though—I go to plenty of parties!"

That was quite true. He had a little goblin friend who lived in the garden outside and often asked him to parties. Sailor always looked smart in his blue trousers, blue sailor-vest with its white-bordered collar, little round hat, black shoes and a whistle on a white thread round his neck.

He loved parties and dancing. He was always going to them and having a good time. "Good-bye!" he would say. "I'm off again! See you at dawn!"

"Get into the ark, get into Noah's ark, there are floods coming!" the sailor doll shouted.

45

Sailor wondered what he could post next. The clockwork mouse's key, of course—and the railway train's key, too—and what about the key that wound up the little motor-car? He would pop each one through the slit in the red money-box—and *how* angry the toys would be!

So he took them all and ran to the money-box. The toys ran after him as soon as they saw what he had got. But down went the three keys into the box, and there they stayed, because the box couldn't be opened unless John, whose box it was, got the key from Mother and unlocked it to take out some of his money. And that might not be for three or four weeks!

"You are wicked, Sailor Doll!" cried Teddy.

"Yes, you really are," cried Golly. "Now we can't ride in the train or the car—and the mouse can't run across the floor."

"I don't care," said the sailor doll, and he didn't. "I'm going to a party tonight. And I shall want a bath before I go, dolls'-house dolls. Get it ready for me!"

"Oh *dear*—that means you'll slop water all over the bathroom floor," said Teeny, the chief dolls'-house doll. "And you always put the mats crooked. You're too big to come into our house."

"I'm coming, all the same," said Sailor, and, sure enough, he squeezed in at the little door that night, squashed his way up the little stairs, and went into the bathroom. Teeny had got the bath ready.

So he took them all and ran to the money-box. The toys ran after him as soon as they saw what he had got.

A lot of whispering went on outside the bathroom door. It was one of the dolls giving a message from Golly to Teeny.

"He says you're to tell Sailor to put his clothes outside the door so that we can give them a good brushing before he goes to the party," whispered the little doll.

"But why *should* we brush his clothes?" whispered back Teeny fiercely. "Horrid creature he is! *I* don't want to brush his clothes!"

"Golly says you're to throw his clothes out of the window and he'll deal with them himself," whispered the tiny doll.

"What's all the whispering about?" shouted Sailor from the bathroom.

"Sailor, throw your things outside the door for brushing," called Teeny.

"Good idea," said Sailor, and out came his blue sailor-vest with its white-bordered collar, his round hat with its ribbon, his blue trousers and his black shoes.

A lot of whispering went on outside the bathroom door.

Teeny threw them out of the window to the golliwog, who was waiting down below. And what *do* you think he did? He didn't brush those clothes. Oh no! He and the other toys took them solemnly to the shelf where the money-box stood, and one by one they posted Sailor's clothes.

"There goes his hat!" said Golly, and posted it.

"There goes his sailor-vest," said Teddy, and posted it.

"There go his shoes," said Angela, and posted them.

47

"And there go his trousers," said the golden-haired doll, and posted those, too!

Sailor had his bath. He got out of it and dried himself. He put on his undervest. Then he yelled for his clothes.

Nobody brought them. He yelled again.

"You can't have them, Sailor," called Teeny. "They're all posted in the money-box."

"What!" shouted Sailor, hardly believing his ears. "Say that again."

"THEY'RE ALL POSTED IN THE MONEY-BOX!" shouted the toys together, and the clockwork mouse gave a squeal of laughter.

Well! Sailor simply didn't know *what* to think. His clothes posted! What was he to wear, then? How could he go to a party without his clothes? He couldn't. Nobody would allow him to go in an undervest. And, anyway, he had terribly skinny legs. He didn't want anyone to see those.

He yelled loudly, "I don't believe you. Bring my clothes at once!"

A large, black head looked in at the window of the bathroom and made Sailor jump. It was Golly, grinning all over his black face.

"Sorry, Sailor. But they really *are* posted. I mean, you love to post *our* things, and we thought it would be great fun to post *yours*. I say, what skinny legs you've got!"

Sailor gave a howl of anger and misery. He believed Golly. He knew his clothes *had* been posted. The toys had done exactly the same to him as he had so often done to them.

And he didn't like it. He didn't like it one bit. "I can't go to the party," he wailed.

He got out and dried himself. He put on his undervest. Then he yelled for his clothes.

"Don't! Don't!" groaned Sailor, and he draped the little towel round
his legs. "Oh, I'm so miserable."

"I can't go out of the dolls'-house. I can't leave this bathroom. I've
only got my vest. Golly, do lend me some clothes."

"Not I," said the golliwog. "You can come out in your vest if you
like. We shan't mind. We shall love to see your skinny legs. I never
knew they were so spindly before. I wish the others could see them."

"Don't! Don't!" groaned Sailor, and he draped the little towel round
his legs. "Oh, I'm so miserable."

"You're only feeling what you made *us* feel," said Golly. "Well, you'll
get your clothes back when we get *our* things back—when the money-box
is opened. Goodness knows when that will be. And I can't *imagine* what
John will say when he sees all the things inside."

I can't either! As for Sailor, he hasn't been to a party for three whole
weeks, he hasn't been out of the dolls'-house for days, and he spends
all the time in the bathroom. He *is* so ashamed of his skinny legs!

Poor Sailor. He'll behave differently when he's got his clothes again,
I'm sure.

THE TWINS GET IN A FIX

THE TWINS were a pair of pickles. They were staying at the seaside, and what a mischievous pair they were! They knocked down other children's sand castles, and took their pails and hid them. They borrowed their shrimping-nets without asking, and they really made the other children very angry.

"Leave our things alone!" they said. "You are most annoying children and we won't play with you if you behave like this."

But the twins took no notice. They always did what they liked.

Now one afternoon the bigger children decided to make an enormous sand castle, the biggest anyone had ever built on the beach. The twins were asked if they would like to help, for such a big castle needed everyone to dig it. But that was too much like hard work for the twins! "No, thank you," said Jim. "We are going shrimping."

"We think sand castles are babyish," said Joan. So they went off by themselves—but they couldn't help watching that sand castle growing!

It really *was* an enormous one! It was the kind that uncles and aunts and fathers and mothers build when they all get together and borrow our spades. Kenneth and Ronnie, Harry and Jack, Lily and Mary, Doris and Freda, all helped to dig it. The castle grew and grew, and the moat around it became wider and wider and deeper and deeper.

"Gracious!" said Kenneth, stopping for a rest. "I really shouldn't think such a big castle has ever been built before! We shall need steps to get up to the top!"

So they cut steps to go up to the top of it. It looked very grand indeed. The children were sorry when tea-time came and they had to go.

"We'll all come back as soon after tea as we can," said Doris. "Then we can take turns at sitting on the top when the tide comes in."

So they hurried home and left the big sand castle. But, you know, as soon as they had gone those twins ran up to look at it—and they walked up the steps right to the very top!

"Oooh!! Isn't it a lovely castle!" said Jim. "Let's call it ours. Let's sit on the top."

"Yes, let's," said Joan. "The tide's coming in, and it will be fun to see it filling the moat and swishing all round the castle."

So the twins sat on the top and watched the waves creeping nearer and nearer. How they screamed with joy when one ran into the moat and lapped all round the castle!

Just then the other children came back, and they shouted with rage when they saw Jim and Joan on the top of their beautiful castle.

"Get down! It's ours!" they cried. "You wouldn't help to build it and you shan't share it!"

"Well, we just *shan't* get down!" said Joan, and she laughed. "And if you try and pull us down we shall kick and knock the castle all to bits. So there!"

"You horrid, nasty children!" said Kenneth. "You know quite well that *we* built this castle, and *we* wanted to sit on the top when the tide came in. Get down at once!"

As soon as they had gone those twins ran up to look—and they walked up the steps.

"The castle is breaking to bits—we'll be in the water!" shouted Jim.

"Shan't! Shan't! Shan't!" sang the twins, and they made rude faces at the others. The children round the castle were very angry, but they couldn't do anything. They were so afraid that Jim and Joan would spoil their lovely castle if they tried to pull them down.

The waves came higher and higher, and the watching children had to run back up the beach. The tide was getting high. They went back and watched their castle.

"We're the kings of the castle, we're the kings of the castle!" sang the twins, and they waved their hands cheekily.

Now that evening the tide was really very high. Big waves swept up to the enormous castle, and lapped all round it every time. Soon the sea was surrounding it, and the waves galloped beyond the castle and up the beach. The castle seemed quite a long way out in the sea.

The twins suddenly looked behind them—and, good gracious, the shore seemed simply miles away! The other children were playing a game of catch-ball and were no longer watching them. It really seemed as if Jim and Joan were far away, alone on a crumbling island in the middle of the big sea.

"Oh!" squealed Joan suddenly, very frightened. "The sea's all round! It's deep, it's deep!"

"The castle is breaking to bits—we'll be in the water!" shouted Jim.

"We'll be drowned, because we can't swim!" yelled Joan. "Help!"

The other children heard the twins shouting, and they looked towards the castle. "It's breaking up and the twins will fall into the deep sea," said Kenneth.

"A jolly good thing!" said Doris. "Let them have a fright!"

"Well, we can't let them drown," said Kenneth. "Where's our boat?"

It was pulled high up on the beach. Kenneth and Jack dragged it down to the water and got into it. They rowed out to the twins, who were now half in the water, standing on what was left of the castle. A big wave came and splashed right over them from top to toe. They nearly fell over. Kenneth reached them just in time.

"This jolly well serves you right!" he said as he dragged them into the boat. "Now, before we take you back to the shore, do you promise to leave our things alone in future—or do you want to be dropped in the sea again?"

"We promise!" sobbed the twins. So Kenneth and Jack rowed them to the beach, and they ran home to change their clothes, cold and hungry.

And did they keep their promise? Yes, they did, because, naughty as they were, they knew that to break a promise is a dreadful thing to do. So now they are much nicer, but they will never sit on top of any sand castle they build. I'm not surprised—are you?

They rowed out to the twins, who were now half in the water, standing on what was left of the castle.

RIDDLE ME REE

My first is in feather but not in down,
My second's in grumble and also in frown,
My third is in blackboard but isn't in chalk,
My fourth is in twig but never in stalk,
My fifth is in weasel and also in stoat,
My sixth is in pig but isn't in goat,
My seventh's in playtime but never in school,
My eighth is in water but isn't in pool,
My ninth is in distance and also beyond,
My whole you will probably find in a pond.

What am I?

Answer on page 174.

STAND ON YOUR OWN FEET

PETER was the boy next door. He was eleven years old, strong and jolly, and always laughing. Ann liked him very much.

Ann was ten, but was small for her age. People thought she was eight. She was shy and timid, and she was so afraid of being scolded for anything that she never owned up when she was in the wrong.

She sat on the wall and watched Peter shooting arrows at a target. "Come and have a try!" said Peter; so she slid down and took the big bow.

"Oh dear—it's so big. It won't spring back and hurt me, will it?"

"Aren't you a little coward!" said Peter, laughing. "Of course it won't. Look—do like this."

It was fun playing with Peter. They took turns at shooting arrows at the target; and then suddenly Ann shot one that went right over the wall! There was a loud miaow and the next-door cat leapt high in the air. The arrow had hit it!

"Oh! Poor thing!" said Peter, and he was over the wall in a trice. But the cat, full of terror, ran away, limping. Peter knew he couldn't catch it. He went back over the wall.

"We'd better go round and knock at Miss Milner's door and tell her you hit the cat by accident," said Peter.

Ann stared at him in the greatest alarm.

What! Go and own up to old Miss Milner, who had a very cross face indeed? Why, she wouldn't know a thing about the cat if nobody told her. So why tell her?

55

"We don't need to say *anything*," said Ann. "She would never know it was one of our arrows that hit her cat. And I don't expect the cat's hurt much, anyway. Miss Milner is *terribly* fierce, you know."

Peter looked fierce, too, quite suddenly. He stared scornfully at Ann.

"Do you know what you are? You're a cowardy custard! Afraid of owning up! The cat *might* be badly hurt—we don't know—and we ought to tell about it. We didn't do it on purpose. Miss Milner will know it was an accident."

"Oh, but, Peter, she'll be so *cross*," said Ann, her eyes filling with tears.

"And what does that matter?" said Peter, still in his horrid, scornful voice. " Have people never been cross with you? Why shouldn't they be sometimes? I feel very cross with you myself. I know it's horrid when people are cross, but even if we don't like it we needn't be *afraid* of it."

"You come with me then, Peter," wept Ann. "*You* tell Miss Milner. And oh, couldn't you say it was *your* arrow that hit the cat? I always feel so scared when things like this happen. You're big and brave, and you're a boy. I'm only a girl, and Mummy says I'm timid and sensitive."

"Timid and sensitive!" said Peter sneeringly. "That's what people often say when their children are cowardly and deceitful. Pooh! And you're only a year younger than I am, and what does it matter if you're a girl? I've

"We don't need to say *anything*," said Ann. "She would never know it was one of our arrows that hit her cat."

56

"You'll grow up into a milk-and-water, namby-pamby, weak
and silly person," went on Peter.

got a cousin of nine called Jean—and she's as good as any boy. She's
coming to stay soon, and I'll be glad to have her. She can stand on her
own feet—*you* always want to stand on somebody else's."

"I don't, I don't," sobbed Ann, thinking that Peter was very unkind.

"You do," said Peter. "When you got into trouble at school you asked
your mother to put it right for you instead of taking your punishment
properly. And when you broke Eileen's ruler in half you were afraid to tell
her. You got George to explain about it to Eileen. And now you want *me*
to go and tell Miss Milner that *I* shot the arrow at the cat. Why can't you
stand on your own feet?"

Ann didn't answer. She wiped her eyes and sniffed.

"You'll grow up into a milk-and-water, namby-pamby, weak and
silly person," went on Peter. "My mother says people like that have never
learned to stand on their own feet and face up to things."

Ann began to cry again. "You don't like me! You won't want to play
with me any more."

Peter looked at Ann and felt sorry for her—but not *too* sorry! No, that would never do. He took her arm and shook it gently.

"Ann! I'm going to tell you something nice now. I do like you. You're fun to play with; and if you'd be brave and stand on your own feet *always*, I'd like you as much as I like any boy. But if you don't stand on your own feet I shan't be friends with you at all. You won't be worth it!"

Ann sniffed again, then wiped her eyes and put away her hanky. She looked at Peter, so straight and tall and fearless. She would never, never be like him—but she could at least *try*. She didn't want him to think Jean was wonderful and play only with her when she came to stay with him. It would be horrid to be left out because she was feeble and silly, and a coward.

"I think you've said horrider things than any grown-up would say," she told him. "But I think perhaps you're right. I don't believe I ever do stand on my own feet. You watch me now!"

The door opened—and there stood the cross-faced Miss Milner.

And to Peter's enormous surprise she went out of his garden and up the front path to Miss Milner's house, where she knocked on the door.

When she heard footsteps coming along the hallway inside she almost ran away. This was the very first time Ann had ever owned up to anything by herself; and although she had felt very brave when she had spoken to Peter, she didn't feel at all brave now.

The door opened—and there stood the cross-faced Miss Milner. "What do you want?" she said.

Ann could hardly get the words out, she was so afraid. "Please—quite by accident

The cat was there in front of the fire. Miss Milner examined her. "She has a little lump on this leg, but that's all," she said.

—I hit your cat with an arrow. I thought I'd better tell you—in case she was hurt. I'm so sorry."

Ann stammered all this out with a very red face, and then turned to run away. But Miss Milner caught hold of her arm.

"Wait!" she said. "Let's have a look at the cat. She's in the kitchen. How *nice* of you to tell me. Most children wouldn't have said a word."

Ann's heart was still beating fast as she went with Miss Milner into her kitchen. The cat was there in front of the fire. Miss Milner examined her.

"She has a little lump on this leg, but that's all," she said. " I don't think she's much hurt. Thank you for telling me. I think a lot of you for that—and when I see your mother I shall tell her what a brave little girl she's got, to come and own up like this."

"Peter made me," said Ann, going red again. "I was afraid to."

"Well, here are biscuits for you both," said Miss Milner, reaching up for a tin. "I made them myself. That boy Peter is grand—absolutely trustworthy. He'll make a fine man, there's no doubt about that !"

59

She raced back to Peter, her face glowing. They munched the biscuits together
whilst Ann told all that had happened.

She gave Ann the biscuits and smiled at her. Ann was astonished. Why, Miss Milner hadn't a cross face after all! She thanked her and raced back to Peter, her face glowing. They munched the biscuits together whilst Ann told all that had happened.

"There you are, you see—as soon as you stand on your own feet things aren't nearly so frightening as you think," said Peter. "But, mind you, even if they *are* frightening it's still no reason for not facing up to them. I must say I never thought you had it in you, Ann, to own up like that!"

Ann thought about many things that night in bed. She remembered a lot, too. She remembered how she had once broken one of the panes in the garden shed and hadn't owned up and Daddy thought it was the garden-boy who had done it. She remembered how she had got into trouble at school over forgotten homework and had begged her mother to go and tell her teacher she hadn't been well and that was why the work wasn't done. And, oh dear, Mother had done what Ann wanted; perhaps Mother didn't know it was wrong not to let her stand on her own feet.

Ann remembered other things. Mother was always making excuses for her. She wouldn't let Daddy scold her when she had broken his fountain-pen. She wouldn't let Granny be cross with her when Ann had left the tap running in the basin and flooded the floor. She hadn't even made Ann go and tell Granny herself—Mother had gone to tell her and explain.

"I've been standing on other people's feet for ages," thought Ann, feeling ashamed. "It's going to be hard to stand on my own now. I hope they'll bear my weight!"

That made her smile. She thought of Peter. However afraid he might be, he always seemed strong and brave and sensible. She wanted him to think well of her. She fell asleep making up her mind that she would be far, far better than his wonderful cousin Jean!

Well, it wasn't at all easy to keep her word to Peter. All kinds of things happened that seemed to make things as difficult as possible.

She lost one of her number books on the way to school, and because she knew she would have to stay in at playtime and get a few sharp words from her teacher she simply could *not* tell her.

She kept thinking what to say and then not saying it. In despair she went to Peter between lessons and told him.

"I'm a coward after all," she said. "I simply *can't* own up!"

"Now you go straight away this minute and say 'Miss Brown, I'm sorry. I must have dropped my number book on the way to school,'" said Peter. "Go on. This very minute. The more you think of it the worse it will be. It's best to do these things AT ONCE."

Peter was right, of course. It was always best to face up to things at once and get them over. Miss Brown wasn't even cross! She put her hand into her desk—and brought

"Now you go straight away this minute to Miss Brown," said Peter. "Go on."

out Ann's number book. "Here it is," she said. "Somebody picked it up and brought it to me. Put your name in it, you know that's the rule."

Ann felt so relieved. How silly she had been to worry herself all the morning! If only she had gone to Miss Brown at once.

The next day she broke one of Mother's vases. Ann was horrified. Still, she knew how to get round Mother. She would wait till Mother found the vase, then she would say she had meant to tell her, and she would cry—and Mother wouldn't scold at all!

"You coward!" Ann said to herself when she had thought all this. "Horrid, deceitful little coward! Go at once and tell Mother."

And she went. Mother was upset, and told Ann she was careless.

"Yes," said Ann. "I *was* careless. Let me buy you another vase out of my own money, Mother."

That made Mother feel very pleased. Ann suddenly felt pleased herself. How nice it was to stand on your own feet! You really did think more of yourself. She felt quite two inches taller!

The next day she broke one of Mother's vases. Ann was horrified. Still, she knew how to get round Mother.

Then Daddy was quite cross because Ann had left her bicycle out in the rain. Usually she would have run to Mother and cried and asked her to tell Daddy she hadn't meant to—but not this time.

"Daddy, I'm sorry," she said. "I absolutely forgot my bike. I'll dry it and clean it this very evening. It won't happen again."

Her father looked at her in surprise. Usually Ann wept buckets of tears, and made all kinds of excuses. This was a new Ann, an Ann he liked very much.

"Spoken like a man!" he said, and Ann went red with pleasure.

Still, things weren't easy at all, because it does take a long time to learn to stand on your own feet when you've been using someone else's for ten years! Ann was often afraid, often quite in despair when things went wrong, and she had somehow to summon up enough courage to face them all by herself. She was determined not to ask Mother or Daddy or Peter to help her in anything. It must be her own feet she stood on and nobody else's!

Her father looked at her in surprise. Usually Ann wept buckets of tears.

Everyone noticed the change in Ann. Only Peter understood it. He was pleased and proud. Proud of himself because he had made Ann into a nicer person, and proud of Ann for being able to find courage to do it.

And then, just before Peter's cousin Jean was due to arrive, something else happened. Ann was out on her bicycle, riding some way behind a small boy. Suddenly a dog ran out and collided with the back wheel of the boy's bicycle. Off he fell at once and lay in the road, squealing with fright and pain.

And what did Ann do? She didn't do what she would have done three weeks before—screamed and ridden away as fast as she could.

No—she rode up to the boy, shooed away the big playful dog, helped up the screaming child, and took him into the nearest house to have his cut knees seen to. She found out his name and address and went riding off to tell his mother and to ask her to come and fetch him home.

Peter heard about it because the boy's mother was a great friend of his own mother's, and told her all about Ann. "A more sensible, helpful child I never saw!" said the little boy's mother. "Stood on her own feet, and did all the right things at once. Now, I do like a child like that."

Peter was bursting with pride. He rushed off to tell Ann. She went red and looked away. She was so pleased to hear Peter's praise that she couldn't say a word.

"I'm glad you're my friend," said Peter. "You really are a friend to be proud of."

"It's a pity Jean's coming tomorrow," said Ann with a sigh. "Just as I'm getting sensible enough to be your friend. Now you'll have Jean and you won't want anyone else to play with."

"Jean will like you awfully," said Peter. "Come and play every day, will you? We'll go for picnics together and go bathing. It'll be fun, the three of us."

It *is* fun. Ann's having a lovely time. She always stands on her own feet now, and what I would dearly like to know is—do you?

She rode up to the boy, shooed away the big playful dog and
helped up the screaming child.

64

The chimpanzees love tea-time—but the
keeper has to see that they behave themselves.
Two of them are up to mischief already, as you
can see!

JIGSAW JOAN

"YOU OUGHT to be called Jigsaw Joan," said George scornfully when Joan began to do yet another jigsaw.

"Well, if I *like* doing jigsaws why shouldn't I do them?" said Joan. "You like collecting stamps and Ronnie likes making things with his Meccano. I don't laugh at you for doing those things whenever you can."

"But you always take up all the table with your silly jigsaws," said Ronnie. "You go on and on. I can't think what you can see in them."

"And I can't see what George sees in his silly stamps, or you see in your endless Meccano," said Joan, beginning to be cross. "Can't you see that some people like doing one thing and some another? I'm good at doing jigsaws, you're good at doing something else. I don't see why we can't all be happy in our own way."

"Well, collecting stamps teaches you geography, so it's some use. And making things with Meccano teaches you to be clever with your hands," said Ronnie. "Doing jigsaws simply doesn't teach you anything."

"I'll do them just for pleasure, then," said Joan, emptying out a box of coloured jigsaw pieces. "And you never know—you might be glad some day that I'm so clever at fitting jigsaws together!"

"We shan't, Jigsaw Joan!" said George. "And remember this: when our birthday comes next week *don't* give us jigsaws. We don't like them."

"I'm not going to," said Joan. "I've got your presents already!"

George's birthday and Ronnie's came very near together—only two days between, so they always shared it and made one big day of it between

The baby bear thinks his big mother is very clever to catch a bun in her mouth! He thinks he will learn that trick as quickly as ever he can!

T-H-B—C

The mouse chewed up the note into about seventy pieces and
made a nest of it in the toy motor-car.

them. Joan didn't give them jigsaws, of course. She gave George a new
stamp-album and Ronnie a book showing him all kinds of different things
he could build.

They were both very pleased. "We've been lucky," they said. "We've
had ships, trains, books—and a ten-shilling note between us!"

"Five shillings each," said George. "Lovely! We're rich!"

"Put the note in your money-box," said their mother. But they forgot
and left it on the window-sill. The wind came and blew it away. It blew
it inside the room and over to the toy cupboard. It blew it right inside
at the very, very back.

So, of course, when the two boys looked for it, it was gone. They
couldn't find it anywhere. They didn't think of looking at the back of the
toy cupboard. They were very sad, but it couldn't be helped. The ten-
shilling note was gone.

Now a little mouse ran in and out of the toy cupboard each night. It
came the night the paper money had blown to the back of the toy cupboard.
It was very pleased to find it there, because it meant to make a paper
nest. This paper would do nicely! It could bite it up into little pieces
and make a cosy little nest in the little toy motor-car.

So it chewed up the note into about seventy pieces and made a nest of
it. But before any babies came into the nest the children's mother turned
out the toy cupboard—and she found the mouse's nest in the toy motor-
car. She called to the children:

"Joan! George! Ronnie! Do come and see. A little mouse has made
a nest in your toy motor-car."

66

They came to look. George gave a cry. "Mother! Look what the nest is made of—our ten-shilling note all bitten into tiny pieces!"

"It's wasted," said Ronnie. "We can't spend it now. Oh, what a pity!"

Joan emptied the tiny bits carefully on to a little tray. She looked at them.

"It's rather like a little paper jigsaw," she said. "If only I could fit all the little bits together properly, and put some sticky paper behind, the ten-shilling note would be whole again and you might be allowed to spend it!"

"Oh, Joan—*could* you do it?" cried George and Ronnie. "Begin now, quickly."

So Joan's deft fingers sorted out the tiny paper bits. She borrowed a new ten-shilling note from Mother to see how it looked, and then she began to do a peculiar jigsaw! A bit here and a bit there. That bit fits there surely, and that one should go there. Here's a straight bit, and here's another!

Joan emptied the tiny bits carefully on to a little tray. She looked at them.
"It's rather like a little paper jigsaw," she said.

"It's coming, it's coming!" cried George. And so it was. It took Joan nearly the whole day to fit the many little bits together and to stick them carefully at the back so that the note showed up whole.

"You're very patient and deft, and very clever, Jigsaw Joan!" said Mother admiringly. "But I don't think anyone would take the note. We'd better go and ask the man at the bank what he thinks."

Well, the man at the bank was very surprised to see such a peculiar note—but he said yes, it was quite all right, he would give each of the boys five shillings for it! What do you think of that?

"We'll never tease you again, Joan, never," said George. "You're the cleverest sister in the world. Come and spend our money with us."

They spent it all—and two shillings and sixpence of it was spent on . . . well, I'll give you a guess! Yes, you're right—it was spent on a new jigsaw for Joan. She's going to do it tonight, and you may be sure she will get every single piece into its right place before she goes to bed. Clever Jigsaw Joan!

The man at the bank was very surprised to see such a peculiar note—but
he said yes, it was quite all right.

LOOK OUT FOR THE ELEPHANT!

"There's an elephant loose!" shouted Jim, rushing into the school playground. "I just heard a man say so. It's escaped from the circus."

"Where is it, where is it?" cried all the children, rushing round Jim.

"It's in the park—and they're afraid it will trample down all the lovely flowers," said Jim.

"Oh, what a shame!" said Sara. She loved flowers, and she couldn't bear to think of the elephant's great feet trampling and breaking them all.

"They've sent for men with sticks," said Jim. "They'll scare that bad elephant properly. I wouldn't mind chasing him myself."

"But elephants are *nice*," said Sara. "I rode on one heaps of times at the zoo. They are gentle and kind. They can't help being big and having enormous feet. I think it's horrid to send for men with sticks!"

"All right, then—*you* go and get the elephant out of the park!" said Jim scornfully. "Go on! See if it will come and eat out of your hand and follow you like a dog! I tell you, big sticks are the only thing to frighten an elephant!"

Sara stood listening to Jim. She was just about to tell him that an elephant *had* eaten out of her hand at the zoo when she had given him a bun—and then a grand idea came into her curly head!

Now when Sara had an idea she always acted on it at once. So she turned and ran into the school. She went to where the eleven-o'clock buns and milk were set ready for the children, and she put twelve of the buns into her school satchel!

You can guess what her idea was now, can't you? Well, well—whoever would think of such a thing? Only Sara!

She ran out of the school gate and made for the park. It wasn't very far away. There was a place in the hedge she could get through. She squeezed through it, and there she was in the park. Where was the elephant?

Well, he wasn't very difficult to see, as you can imagine. There he stood, waving his enormous trunk to and fro, his great feet very near to a big bed of glorious dahlias.

In the distance Sara could hear shouting, and she guessed that men were coming with sticks.

"They'll only scare him and he'll go galloping over the dahlias," thought Sara. "I'd better hurry."

So she trotted down the path to where the big elephant stood. She went right up to him.

"You're awfully like the elephant who gave me rides at the zoo," she told him, and he looked down at her out of little, twinkling eyes. He flapped his ears and made a little trumpeting noise.

"Are you asking for a bun?" said Sara, and she put her hand in her satchel. "Well, here's one."

The elephant put out his trunk and took the bun. He swung his trunk up to his big mouth—and the bun was gone! He held out his trunk for another.

"Well, you can have all my buns if you come quietly down this path with me," said Sara, "away from

The elephant put out his trunk and took the bun. He swung his trunk up to his mouth.

The elephant, seeing that she had plenty more buns, followed her
closely, trying to put his trunk inside the satchel.

these lovely flower-beds. Your feet are so big, you know. Here you
are, here's another bun."

She gave him another, and then began to walk down the path to the
park-gate. The elephant, seeing that she had plenty more buns, followed
her closely, trying to put his trunk inside the satchel.

Sara laughed. "Oh, you wait till I give you one! There you are. Now
do come along. We'll soon be at the gate."

Well, well, well! The men with sticks stopped at once when they saw
the elephant following little Sara like a dog.

"Look at that!" they said. "That kid has got old Jumbo eating out of
her hand! Send his keeper to that park-gate—that will be the place to
capture the elephant. He's not scared any more, or angry. Well, would
you believe it!"

Jumbo followed Sara all the way to the gate, eating the buns she gave
him—and there at the gate was the elephant's keeper waiting for him!
Jumbo was very glad indeed to see him. He loved his keeper.

Holding her there with his trunk, he set off down the road that led
past the school, swaying this way and that.

"Thank you, little girl," said the keeper gratefully. "If it hadn't
been for you, poor old Jumbo would have been sent racing all over the
flower-beds in fright, and he might have done a lot of damage. Now—is
there any reward you'd like for getting him to come quietly?"

"Well," said Sara, "I suppose—I suppose I couldn't ride on his head,
could I, right past our school? The children would hardly believe it if
they saw me there!"

"Yes. Old Jumbo will set you on his head and hold you there with his
trunk," said the keeper with a laugh. "Hup, Jumbo, hup!"

Jumbo picked up Sara very gently and set her on his big head. Then,
holding her there with his trunk, he set off down the road that led past
the school, swaying this way and that.

"Look! LOOK! It's Sara up there!" shouted the children. "Hurrah
for Sara! Sara, how did you get there? Oh, SARA!"

It was a lovely reward, wasn't it? She deserved it, though, because
she really did have a very good idea!

MAKE A DANCING CLOWN

HERE is a little toy you can make very easily and which will give you and your friends many amusing hours.

Just trace out the little clown, transfer it to a piece of fairly thick card and then cut it out.

Now cut out the two circles in the base of the figure.

That wasn't very difficult, was it?

Now colour him with the brightest paints in your box and he is finished.

Slip your fingers through the holes and off he will go dancing merrily!

IT CAME BACK TO HIM IN THE END

IT ALL began when Tom did a bad and foolish thing. He was sitting on the bus-stop seat with two boys, waiting for the bus to take him home.

On the other end of the seat was old Mrs. Trent, nodding her head, almost asleep, as she waited for the bus, too. Beside her was a full basket of shopping.

One of the boys nudged Tom. "I say, look—do you see what the old lady has got at the top of her basket?"

Tom looked. Mrs. Trent had bought a bar of chocolate cream for her grandson, and there it was, at the very top of the basket.

"Take it," whispered the boy to Tom. "She's asleep and she won't know. I dare you to!"

Now dares are silly, of course—they are always meant to make you do bad or dangerous things, and you have to be very brave and wise to say no.

Tom wasn't wise, nor was he brave enough to say he wouldn't take the dare. So he edged up slowly to old Mrs. Trent, hoping that the bus would come before he could do such a bad thing. Tom wasn't really bad. He just wanted to show the other boys that he was daring enough to do what they said.

He put his hand into the basket. His fingers closed over the bar of chocolate. He lifted it out gently. And then something happened.

A big dog came bounding up and knocked against him playfully. The chocolate flew out of his hand and landed on the ground. The dog pounced on it at once!

It cracked the bar in half, paper and all—and at that very moment, when the dog had the chocolate bar in his mouth, old Mrs. Trent woke up! She saw the dog eating her precious bar of chocolate and was very angry indeed.

She picked up her umbrella and began to whip the dog. Biff, biff, whack! Biff! WHACK!

The dog yelped in pain. The three boys looked on in horror. Tom was as red as a beetroot. It was all his fault that the dog was being beaten; but although he had been bold enough to do what the other boys had dared him to, he wasn't brave enough to own up. So he just watched whilst the dog was beaten.

Ah, Tom—you've started a horrid chain of happenings that will all come back to you in the end. You wait and see!

Up came the owner of the dog, a little fierce-eyed woman. "How dare you beat my dog like that! Put your umbrella down at once, I tell you! The poor creature, you've almost broken his back. It's a wonder he didn't fly at you."

"He stole a chocolate bar out of my basket!" cried Mrs. Trent. "He's a thief-dog! Taking things out of people's baskets!"

"I'm sure he never did," said the other woman, patting her dog gently. "He has never stolen anything in his life. Never! You just say you're sorry for beating my dog or I'll do something to *make* you sorry."

"I'm not apologising to a dog, so there!" said old Mrs. Trent, gathering up her things as she saw the bus coming. "And, what's more, you can't make me *feel* sorry, either!"

"How dare you beat my dog like that! Put your umbrella down at once, I tell you!"

75

"Oh, can't I!" called the other woman as Mrs. Trent got on the bus. "Well, I can! You get the fish-scraps for your cat from my shop, don't you? Well, you won't get any more!"

You see, she was Mrs. Kipps, who kept the only fish-shop in the village. Every other day she packed up a nice little parcel of fish-scraps for Mrs. Trent's big tabby-cat, and Mrs. Trent fetched them. The cat loved the scraps and always waited impatiently for them to be cooked.

"I told you I'd not save you any more because you beat my dear old dog."

Mrs. Kipps turned to the three boys, who were just getting on the bus, too. "I'll teach her to say my dog steals!" she cried. "Why, she'll be saying next that *you* steal!"

That made Tom go redder than ever. He was really ashamed of himself. So were the other boys. But the thing was done, and hadn't been put right by Tom when it could have been.

Mrs. Kipps was as good as her word. She gave all her fish-scraps to Mr. Morris for his Siamese cats. There wasn't a scrap for Mrs. Trent when she called.

"I told you I'd not save you any more because you beat my dear old dog," said Mrs. Kipps firmly. "You can buy good fish for your cat from now on. Instead of two penny-worth of scraps you'll have to buy a shilling's-worth of fish."

"I can't afford it," said Mrs. Trent. "You know I can't."

"You should have thought of that before you beat my dog and called him a thief," said Mrs. Kipps. "Next customer, please."

76

The lids would fall to the ground and then the cat would leap
nimbly into the bin and sniff about for odd scraps.

Well, Mrs. Trent went home without her usual fish-scraps. Her tabby-cat met her at the door and was surprised not to smell fish. It mewed loudly.

"None for you today, poor puss," said Mrs. Trent. "I'll give you what tit-bits I can from my own food, but it won't be much! You'll have to do a little hunting on your own and feed yourself."

The cat waited about for the fish, but it got none because there was none to get. Mrs. Trent put down bits and pieces, but the cat was a large one and was always hungry. It grew thin and starved-looking, and hunted about in the rubbish-heaps for food.

Then it smelt at the dustbins. People put all kinds of things in there, the cat knew that. If only it could move the lids it could get into the bins and scrape about for odds and ends of food.

Well, it was a big cat and a clever one. It soon learnt how to shift the dustbin lids. Crash! They would fall to the ground and then the cat would leap nimbly into the bin and sniff about for odd scraps.

77

And then the rat found out that the cat went round the dustbins, jerking off the lids and eating the scraps. The rat was pleased.

Now one day a rat came to that district. It was a big one, but rather thin, because it had not found much food the last week or two. It smelt the cat and was afraid. It hid under the floor of a garden shed one night, after it had smelt the cat around, and listened to find out where the cat lived. The rat didn't want to live anywhere near it.

And then the rat found out that the cat went round the dustbins, jerking off the lids and eating the scraps inside. The rat was pleased.

"I've never been able to move a dustbin lid," he thought. "This is grand! I'll wait till the cat leaves one dustbin and goes to the next, and then I'll pop into each one after her, as soon as she's gone, and finish up what she's left!"

Well, that is exactly what he did, and before long he became very plump and well-fed indeed. Each night he followed the cat around at a safe distance, feeding from the dustbins whose lids she had taken off.

Now the rat began to think it would be a very good idea to take a rat wife for himself and have some young rats. "I could always find plenty of food for them in the dustbins," he thought. "Yes, I'll go and find a nice young rat and ask her to be my wife."

So very soon another rat came to join him and made a cosy nest of paper and wood shavings under the floor of the garden shed.

Ten young rats were born, all lively and strong. The big rat was pleased, and so was his wife. "Soon we shall cover this district with rats," said he. "Nobody likes us, but I don't care! As long as the cat takes off the dustbin lids for us we are all right for food."

But soon people grew tired of hearing the crash of dustbin lids in the night, and they set a watch for the cat. Mr. Wilton caught her and looked at her.

"It's Mrs. Trent's cat! She must lock it in the house at night. We can't have it taking off our dustbin lids and scraping about in the rubbish each night. It just won't do!"

So Mrs. Trent had to keep her old cat in the house at night—and there was no more crashing of dustbin lids at midnight and no more stealing of dustbin food!

And that meant that the rat couldn't find the food either! He was surprised and annoyed when he found all the dustbin lids on at night. No more scraps for him! No more tit-bits for his wife and children either.

"It's no good asking the cat why she doesn't go round the bins at night any more," he told his wife. "She would just snap me up. Cats are like that!"

"Well, you will have to go round and see what you can find," said his wife. "We've ten children now and it will be hard to feed them. Hunt well."

No more scraps for him! No more tit-bits for his wife and children either.

The rat hunted all night long, but all he found was a few crumbs of biscuit dropped by a child, and an old potato skin.

"This won't do for our large family!" said his wife. "You must do better than this! Are there no young chicks or ducklings you can find? There are often plenty at this time of year. Go to the farm and see."

Now Tom's father kept a farm not far off. Tom loved the farm. He loved all the animals on it—the horses, the cows, the sheep, the ducks, the pigs, and even the old turkeys that said "gobble, gobble" in deep voices whenever he passed.

This year he had ten little yellow ducklings of his own—dear little things a few days old, hatched out by an old mother hen. She had the ten ducklings in a coop with her and kept guard over them day and night.

And one night the rat smelt them out! He crept up and put his nose between the bars of the coop. The mother hen pecked it at once and he drew back.

"Cheep," said a duckling, and put its head out from beneath the hen's wing.

"Cluck," said the hen warningly, and the duckling drew it back. But the rat had seen it!

He went back home to his wife. "There are ducklings at the farm, with a silly hen to keep watch," he said. "I'll soon have them!"

He crept up and put his nose between the bars of the coop. The mother hen pecked it at once and he drew back.

He was sly and cunning. He found a tiny hole at the back of the coop and gnawed away at it till he had made it big enough to slip through. The mother hen did not hear anything. The rat saw a tiny webbed foot sticking out from under the hen's feathers and pounced on it. With a frightened cheep the duckling awoke—but before the hen could do anything the rat had gone off with the duckling!

He came back for another that night, and yet another. The hen clucked and squawked, but the rat was too clever for her.

Now when Tom went to see his ducklings the next day there were only seven. He was very upset. What could have happened to the others? Had a rat got them? He would move the coop to another place!

But the rat soon found out where the coop had been moved to, and a night or two later he went to the mother hen again. She was awake at once. She clucked loudly and turned herself round to peck at him.

When Tom went to see his ducklings the next day there were only seven.

In a trice the rat was round at the front of the coop, in between the bars, before the hen had even had time to turn herself round! He dragged out a cheeping duckling, and went back for another. He got a peck on the back, but he didn't mind that. He carried off the ducklings, and his wife was full of delight.

By the end of the week not a single duckling was left, not one. The rat had had them all. Tom went to his mother with tears in his eyes.

81

"There's none left now," he told her. "Oh, Mother, I do feel so miserable. They were such lovely ducklings, and I was going to let them grow into beautiful big ducks and lay eggs for me to sell. They would be my very own."

"It's a shame, Tom," said his mother.

"It's not fair," said Tom. "What have I done to have such a horrid thing happen to me? I haven't done anything at all!"

Oh, but you have, Tom! Have you forgotten when you were dared to take that bar of chocolate out of old Mrs. Trent's basket? Have you forgotten how she beat Mrs. Kipps' dog for stealing it and you didn't say a word? You didn't guess that because of that Mrs. Kipps wouldn't save her fish-scraps for Mrs. Trent's cat, and so her cat learnt to push off dustbin lids and look for scraps. You didn't know that a rat came and helped himself to scraps, too, from the dustbins and took a wife and raised a hungry family.

You didn't guess that when the cat was locked up at night and couldn't take off the dustbin lids the rat went looking somewhere else for food, and found your dear little ducklings. It was all because of something *you* did, Tom, that your ducklings were stolen and killed.

Poor Tom! I feel sorry for him, don't you? He really didn't know that one wrong deed will set a whole lot of other wrongs going round the world, and will often come back to the one who starts them. Well—I'm going to be very, very careful—aren't you? I think I'll set a good deed going, not a bad one!

Now then, Busy-Body

Busy-Body, the brownie, was always poking his nose into everything. He knew everybody's business and told everybody's secrets. He was a perfect little nuisance.

He peeped here and he poked there. If Dame Twig had a new hen he knew all about it. If Mister Hallo had a new hat he knew exactly what it was like and where he had got it from. He was a real little busybody, so his name was a very good one.

One day Madam Soapsuds came to live in Chestnut Village, where Busy-Body had his cottage. She brought with her a small van, labelled "Laundry Goods. With Very Great Care". She wouldn't let the removal men unpack this van. No, it had to be stood in her front garden and left there till she herself unpacked it.

Busy-Body was very curious, of course. Why should Madam Soapsuds want to unpack this little van herself? Was there something magic in it that she didn't want anyone else to see? He decided to hide himself under a bush in the front garden and watch till Madam Soapsuds took out what was in that little van.

That night, before the moon was up, Madam Soapsuds came out into the garden. She went to the van. But before she opened the door she stood still and said a little magic rhyme:

"If anyone is hiding
They must go a-riding
On this witch's stick.

He sat on the stick, though he tried hard not to, and then up he
went into the air, very frightened.

And she threw an old broomstick down on the ground. Poor Busy-
Body found his legs taking him from under his bush over to the stick!
He sat on the stick, though he tried hard not to, and then up he went into
the air, very frightened.

"Ho, ho!" said Madam Soapsuds, pleased. "I had an idea you were
trying to poke your silly little nose into my business, Busy-Body. Better
keep away from me. I keep my own secrets!"

So, whilst Busy-Body rose higher and higher into the air, clinging for
dear life to his broomstick, Madam Soapsuds quietly and quickly unpacked that secret little van, and nobody saw her.

Busy-Body had a dreadful night. For one thing it was windy and cold,
and for another thing he wasn't used to riding broomsticks. It was most
uncomfortable, and was also very jerky, so that he had to cling tightly.
He felt sure the stick was jerking him on purpose.

When the sun came up the broomstick went down. It landed on Busy-
Body's roof, and he had to climb down from there, very stiff and cold.

He was also very angry. How *dare* Madam Soapsuds treat him like that! He'd find out all her secrets, he would, he would!

Madam Soapsuds told everyone what had happened to Busy-Body, and they laughed. "How do you like riding at night?" they asked him. "Did you have to click to your broomstick to make it gallop?"

Busy-Body scowled. He hoped that nobody would like Madam Soapsuds. But they did like her—and very much, too. She ran a fine laundry, and was very cheap. The folks of Chestnut Village could take a bag of washing to her in the morning and have it all back, washed, mangled, dried and ironed, at tea-time. It was really wonderful.

She wouldn't let anyone watch her at work. "No," she said, "I like to work alone, thank you. I like to do it my own way."

"She's got some magic at work," said Busy-Body to everyone. "That's what she's got. She couldn't do all that washing by herself. Nobody could. Why, she had seven bags of dirty linen to wash today, and all the blankets from Dame Twig, seven of them. And, hey presto, by tea-time they were all clean, dry and ironed! She's got some wonderful washing secret, no doubt about that."

Busy-Body longed to find out the secret. It must be some magic machinery, perhaps. Or hundreds of tiny imp servants. Perhaps they had been hidden in that van, the night he had gone broomstick-riding. Busy-Body couldn't sleep at night

"She's got some magic at work," said Busy-Body to everyone.

WASHING
ROOM
·
DANGER

"Can't I just go inside and see what happens?"
asked her friend Dame Twig.

because he puzzled his brains so hard about Madam Soapsuds.

Madam Soapsuds had one big room in her house that nobody went into. She called it her Washing Room. Queer noises went on there—clinkings and splashings and bumpings.

"Can't I just go inside and see what happens?" asked her friend Dame Twig. But Madam Soapsuds shook her head.

"No. It would be dangerous. Not even I go into that room, Dame Twig. I just shake all the dirty linen out of the bag, fling it into the room, shut the door and leave it. At tea-time I open the door, and there is the linen, all clean and dry and ironed, piled up neatly for me to take."

"Extraordinary," said Dame Twig. "Well, Madam Soapsuds, watch out for Busy-Body. He'll be poking his nose into that room if he can."

"He'll be sorry if he does," said Madam Soapsuds.

Busy-Body certainly meant to find out the secret of that Washing Room. He watched Madam Soapsuds from the window of his cottage opposite every single day. He knew she went shopping for an hour on Monday. She went for a walk on the common on Tuesday. She shopped again on Wednesday. She gave her friends tea on Thursday. She went to tea with one or other of the villagers on Friday. And on Saturday she went out for the whole day to her sister in the next village.

"That's the day for me to go to her house," thought Busy-Body. "She's away all day! I could get into her sitting-room window, because she always leaves it a little bit open. Oho, Madam Soapsuds, I'll soon find out your secret and tell everyone! I'm sure it's one you're ashamed of, or you wouldn't be so careful to hide it!"

That Saturday Madam Soapsuds put on her best bonnet and shawl as usual, took a basket of goodies, and went to catch the bus to the next village. Busy-Body watched her get into the bus.

He stole out of his cottage and went round to the back of Madam Soapsuds' little garden. Nobody was about. He climbed over the fence and made his way to the back of the house, hiding in the bushes so that nobody would see him.

The sitting-room window was just a bit open as usual. He slid it up. Then he jumped inside. From the Washing Room he could hear curious noises.

Slishy-sloshy, splish-splash-splosh. Creak-clank, creak! Flap-flap-flap! Drippitty, drip! Bump-bump-bump! He stood and listened to the noises, filled with curiosity. He *must* peep inside that door and see what was happening.

He went to the door. It was shut. He turned the handle and the door opened a little way. A puff of steam came out in his face.

He slid up the sitting-room window and jumped inside. From the Washing Room he could hear curious noises.

87

Busy-Body carefully put his head round the door, but he couldn't see a thing because it was so steamy just there. He listened to the noises. Whatever could be making them?

He pulled the door open wide and went cautiously inside. The door at once slammed shut. Busy-Body turned in fright and tried to open it. But he couldn't. Ooooh!

The steam cleared a little. Then he saw that the room was full of tubs of hot and cold water, full of steam that swirled about, full of mangles that swung their rollers round fast and creaked and clanked, full of hot irons that bumped their way over tables on which clothes were spreading themselves ready to be pressed.

There was nobody there. Everything was working at top speed by itself. The soap in the tubs made a tremendous lather, the scrubbing-brushes worked hard, the mangles pressed the water from clothes, the whirling fan that dried them rushed busily round and round up in the ceiling.

Busy-Body felt scared. He had never seen so much magic at work at once. Look out, Busy-Body, look out! You shouldn't be in that room. The magic is too strong. He felt himself pushed towards one of the tubs. Then in he went, splash, into the hot water. A big piece of soap ran all over him and made a big lather, and he began to splutter because there was so much soap in his eyes and nose.

He felt himself pushed towards one of the tubs. Then in he went, splash, into the hot water. A big piece of soap ran all over him.

He was flung up to the ceiling, where he hung on a wire to dry
in the wind made by the magic fan.

"Stop! Stop!" begged Busy-Body. But the magic couldn't stop. It was set to go, and go it had to. Besides, it wanted to. It didn't often have somebody to wash, mangle and iron. It usually only had clothes. Poor Busy-Body! He was soused in tub after tub, soaped and re-soaped, lathered, and scrubbed till he felt as if he was nothing but a bit of rag.

Then he was shot over to one of the mangles whose rollers were turning busily, squeezing the water out of the clothes. Look out, Busy-Body.

He just managed to fling himself down below the mangle before he was put in between the rollers. He crawled into a corner and wept bitterly. Why had he bothered about Madam Soapsuds' horrid secret?

A tub came near him, and he was splashed into water again. It was cold water this time. How horrid! Then he was flung up to the ceiling, where he hung on a wire to dry in the wind made by the magic fan. But he couldn't bear that and he flung himself down, dripping wet.

Look-out, Busy-Body! You are near the magic irons! Wheeeee! He was up on the ironing table, and a hot iron ran over his leg. Busy-Body

89

squealed and leapt off the table. Into a butt of hot water he went this time, and a big scrubbing-brush began to scrub him in delight. Then he was flung into a tub of cold water and rinsed well.

He went too near a mangle again and nearly got squeezed. He just managed to get away in time, weeping bitterly.

"I've never been so wet in my life! I've never had so much soap in my mouth and nose and eyes! Oh, how can I get away?"

"Good gracious! What's this?" said Madam Soapsuds, in surprise and anger.

It was lucky for Busy-Body that Madam Soapsuds happened to come home early that day or he would most certainly have been mangled and ironed sooner or later. But suddenly the door opened, and a voice said:

"I have come for you, clothes!"

And at once all the cleaned, dried, mangled, ironed clothes put themselves in neat piles beside the door—and on top poor Busy-Body was flung, wet and dripping!

"Good gracious! What's this?" said Madam Soapsuds, in surprise and anger. "*You*, Busy-Body! Serves you right for peeping and prying. You're not dry or mangled or ironed. Go back and be done properly."

"No, no!" squealed Busy-Body, afraid. "Let me go. Let me go!"

Madam Soapsuds got hold of him. He was dripping from head to foot.

"I'm going to shut up my Washing Room now," she said. "So you can't be dried there after all. I'll peg you up on my line in the garden."

"He poked his nose into what didn't concern him," said Madam Soapsuds.
"He's got a lot of secrets to tell."

And to Busy-Body's shame and horror she pegged him firmly up on her clothes-line by the seat of his trousers—and there he swung in the wind, unable to get away. Everybody came to look and laugh.

"He poked his nose into what didn't concern him," said Madam Soapsuds. "He's got a lot of secrets to tell. But if he tells them he'll go back into my Washing Room to learn a few more! Are you dry, Busy-Body?"

Busy-Body was so ashamed and unhappy that he cried tears into the puddle made by his dripping clothes. Nobody felt very sorry for him. Busybodies are always punished by themselves in the end!

"Now you can go," said Madam Soapsuds, unpegging him. "And what are you going to do? Are you going to run round telling my secrets?"

No. Busy-Body wasn't going to do anything of the sort. He didn't even want to *think* of that awful Washing Room. So he tried not to.

But he can't help dreaming about it, and when the neighbours hear him yelling at night they laugh and say: "He thinks he's in that Washing Room again. Poor Busy-Body!"

10 LITTLE KITTEN·CATS

Ten little kitten-cats, walking in a line,
One chased his curly tail, then there were nine.
Nine little kitten-cats, rising rather late,
One forgot to wash himself, then there were eight.
Eight little kitten-cats, lapping cream from Devon,
One over-ate himself, then there were seven.
Seven little kitten-cats, up to naughty tricks,
One was smacked and sent to bed, then there were
six.
Six little kitten-cats, peeping in a hive,
One was stung upon his nose, then there were five.
Five little kitten-cats, looking round the door,
One ran out and lost himself, then there were four.
Four little kitten-cats, climbing up a tree,
One was pecked by sparrows, then there were
three.
Three little kitten-cats, wondering what to do,
One went to play with Bobs, then there were two.
Two little kitten-cats, yawning in the sun,
One yawned himself away, then there was one.
This one little kitten-cat—Bimbo is his name—
Ran away to live with me—and that's how he
came!

Can you draw this poem?

"Quick! Save Me!"

THERE were once five children, who always played together in the fields. Their names were John, Betty, Alan, Mary and Colin.

Colin was the smallest, and because he was not so big as the others his mother always told them to be sure and look after him well.

"Now see that he doesn't fall down," said his mother. "And don't let him climb trees. Do watch over him carefully, because he is only a little boy."

"We'll look after him, Mrs. Brown," promised the bigger children. "Come along, Colin."

Colin felt very important at having to be looked after so carefully. He thought it would be fun to pretend to be in trouble and shout for help. Then he would see all the other children rushing to his help.

So when they were not looking he slipped through a gap in the hedge and went to climb a tree. When he was half-way up he smiled to himself and began to shout for help.

"Help! Save me! Help!"

"Good gracious! That's Colin calling!" cried Mary. "Quick! He's in trouble!"

All the children squeezed through the hedge, scratching their arms and tearing their clothes.

"Quick! Save me!" shouted Colin, really enjoying himself. The children tore to the tree.

"Poor Colin!" cried Betty. "Are you hurt?"

93

"Save me, save me!" shouted Colin.

"He doesn't *look* hurt," said Alan. "And what did he climb a tree for? He knows his mother said he wasn't to."

The children got Colin down. "You could really have climbed down yourself," said John. "Now for goodness' sake keep with us."

The children kept a sharp eye on Colin for the rest of the morning and he couldn't slip away. But the next day he thought it would be great fun to try the same trick again. So this time he slipped off and ran to the bank of the river. He climbed down over the bank and crouched by the water. The others couldn't see him.

Then he began to shout for help. "Save me! Help! Help! Oh, save me, save me!"

The other children looked up. "My goodness, he must be in the river!" cried John. "Come on, quick!"

They tore to the river, and there they found Colin, crouching down by the bank, laughing.

"What do you mean by calling for help when there's nothing the matter?" said John, hauling Colin up the bank rather roughly. "You're just silly, the way you shout for nothing!"

Colin grinned. He really thought it was a very good joke, and he made up his mind he would play the same trick again. So the next morning off

They tore to the river, and there they found Colin, crouching down
by the bank, laughing.

he went and climbed to the top of a haystack. He could easily get down, but he would pretend that he couldn't. So there he lay shouting and shouting.

"Help! I'm in trouble! Come and save me! I shall fall!"

"Bother! That's Colin shouting again," said Betty, dropping her skipping-rope. "What's he doing *now*?"

All the children tore about looking for Colin. "Help! Oh, help!" he cried. At last they saw him on the haystack, and they looked at him crossly.

"What's the matter?" they said.

"I shall fall, I shall fall!" shouted Colin.

"Oh no you won't," said

All the children tore about looking for Colin.
At last they saw him on the haystack.

Mary. "We know that haystack very well—you can easily get up and down it from the other side. Get down yourself before we pull you down, you naughty, shouting boy!"

Colin slid down the other side. The other children scolded him, but he didn't mind. He was having great fun, pretending to be in trouble.

Two days later Colin slipped away again and went to hide in the farm-yard. He would shout and shout from there, and the children would have to come quite a long way to find him. Good!

He crouched down behind a fence—but, oh dear, what was this? It was a large goose looking at him round the corner! "S-s-s-s-s!"

Then another goose came up, and another and another. Colin crouched back against the wall, very much frightened. The first goose pecked at his socks.

"Oh, don't!" cried Colin. "Don't peck me! John, Mary, come quickly!"

95

The other children heard him shouting, and they looked at one another and smiled. "Little silly!" John said. "He's always shouting for nothing. He's playing a trick on us again. Well, we just won't go this time."

"No, we just won't," said Mary.

So they didn't go and find Colin. He yelled and shouted and shouted and yelled, but nobody came at all. The big geese pecked his socks and pecked his shoes and one of them even pecked his handkerchief out of his pocket!

"S-s-s-s-s-s-s-s!" they said. "Cackle, cackle!"

At last Colin got away from the big geese and ran sobbing and crying to the other children. They looked at him in surprise.

"What's the matter?" they said.

"The g-g-geese have p-p-pecked me to b-bits," he sobbed. "And you d-didn't come and save me."

"Well, it's your own fault, Colin," said John. "You were always shouting for nothing—and how could we tell you were *really* in trouble when you shouted this time? Just don't do it again, and we'll always come to you."

So now Colin never shouts for nothing—and wasn't his mother cross to see his spoilt shoes and socks!

He yelled and shouted and shouted and yelled,
but nobody came at all.

96

"Keep still while I give you your morning wash!" says the mother giraffe to her long-legged baby. "Soon your neck will be long enough to look over the railings!"

JIFFY gets into TROUBLE

R. TYNDALL.

WHEN LITTLE Sing-Song came up the lane throwing her new ball into the air Jiffy hid behind a hedge in his garden and watched her.

Sing-Song was singing as usual as she threw her ball up and caught it.

"Up you go,
Ever so high.
If I'm not careful
You'll touch the sky!"

And at the last line little Sing-Song sent the ball up very high indeed. She hardly ever caught it when she threw it so high, and then it bounced and she had to run after it, laughing.

"Down you go
And you bounce away.
'You can't catch me!'
I can hear you say!"

Jiffy watched for Sing-Song to throw up her ball again. She was near his hedge. Suppose she missed it and it bounced into his garden—he could get it before she did and keep it. She wouldn't know!

Up went the ball again, and Sing-Song began her funny little song once more.

"Up you go,
Ever so high,
If I'm not careful
You'll touch the sky!"

How very pretty the baby llama is! No wonder its mother and father are proud of it. It will stay close to them while it is so young, and can run as fast as its parents.

97

T-H-B—D

And at the last line she sent the ball so high into the air that for one moment Jiffy really thought it *might* touch the sky. But it didn't, of course. It began to fall, and, to Jiffy's delight, it came over his garden. He reached out his hands and caught it!

Sing-Song didn't see him, because he was behind the bush. She opened the gate and ran in.

"Mrs. Jiffy, Mrs. Jiffy!" she called. "Can I come in and get my ball?"

"Of course!" called Jiffy's mother from the cottage. "Come in, little Sing-Song."

But when Sing-Song came in she couldn't find the ball anywhere. That wasn't surprising, because Jiffy had hidden it under the bush. He came out grinning.

His mother saw him. "Jiffy! Now, Jiffy, *you* haven't got Sing-Song's ball, have you? Because if you have you must give it to her. Don't be naughty, now."

"I haven't got it," said Jiffy.

It began to fall, and, to Jiffy's delight, it came over his garden. He reached out his hands and caught it!

"Well, you go and borrow Mr. Trinky's big, long stick," said his mother.
"You can easily reach the ball with that."

But still his mother wasn't certain. She knew Jiffy wasn't always very truthful, and it made her sad. She looked at him sharply.

"Well, you look hard for it," she said. "And I'll come and look, too!"

Jiffy was alarmed. He didn't want his mother to come and look for the ball. She would be certain to find it under the bush—and she would guess he had hidden it there. So he told a story.

"I know where it is," he said. "I saw it fall. It fell on our roof and rolled into the gutter that goes round it to catch the rain."

"Well, you go and borrow Mr. Tinky's big, long stick," said his mother. "You can easily reach the ball with that. Can you wait till he borrows the stick, Sing-Song?"

"No, I'm afraid I can't," said Sing-Song. "My mother is waiting for me to catch the bus with her. But perhaps Jiffy could leave the ball at our house if he gets it out of the gutter for me? Goodbye!"

She skipped off, singing one of her little songs.

> "My ball is lost,
>   Oh, what a pity!
>   It really was
>   So very pretty!"

"Funny little singing thing," said Mrs. Jiffy, smiling after Sing-Song. "Jiffy, what are you standing there like that for? Didn't you hear me tell you to go and borrow Mr. Tinky's big stick?"

Now Mr. Tinky lived a long way away, and Jiffy didn't want to go and borrow a stick to poke at a gutter for a ball that wasn't there. But he

99

He pretended to go. He went out of the front gate and then crept in again
at the back, and sat in the shed, reading.

couldn't tell his mother that. So he pretended to go. He went out
of the front gate and then crept in again at the back and sat in the shed
reading. When he thought it was about time for him to say he was back
from Mr. Tinky's he put down his book and strolled into the house.

"Oh—so there you are," said his mother. "Where is Mr. Tinky's
stick?"

Jiffy made up a story at once. He was clever at that! "Oh, Ma, Mr.
Tinky's sorry, but he had burglars last night, and he broke his stick
chasing them away."

"Well, I never! Burglars! And how brave of old Mr. Tinky to chase
them away!" said his mother. "Dear me! Well, Jiffy, you must go along
to Mrs. Gobbo and ask her to lend you her step-ladder. She's got a nice
big one. Mine's too small."

"Blow!" said Jiffy to himself. He wanted to read his book. He didn't
want to borrow a step-ladder to find a ball that was still safely under
the bush! So he did exactly the same thing again—walked out of the
front gate and crept in again at the back.

In twenty minutes' time he came out of the shed! "Ma! Mrs. Gobbo's
sorry, but she says—er—she says that poor Mr. Gobbo climbed up on the
step-ladder yesterday and it broke and he fell off and hurt his back. So
she can't lend it to anyone till it's mended."

"Good gracious me! I do hope poor old Gobbo isn't badly hurt," said Mrs. Jiffy in surprise. "What a sad thing! Well, Jiffy, you must go to Mr. Tock now and ask him for that ladder of his. It's far too long, of course, but that won't matter. It will be rather heavy for you to carry, but you're a strong boy. Go along and get the ladder."

This was too bad! "First it's a stick; then it's a step-ladder, now it's a ladder!" groaned Jiffy to himself. "Why ever did I tell that story about Sing-Song's ball being in the gutter? It's made me tell bigger and bigger stories all the morning. Well—I suppose I'd better pretend to get Mr. Tock's ladder! But I only hope this is the last thing Ma wants me to fetch!"

He went out of the front gate and crept in at the back for the third time. He took up his book again. He was quite lost in it, and read for a long time. Then he heard his mother calling.

"Jiffy! Jiffy! Aren't you back from Mr. Tock's yet? Where's the ladder?"

Jiffy ran out of the shed in a hurry, trying to think of something to tell his mother.

"Oh, Ma, yes—here I am. But I couldn't borrow his ladder. He's painting his house, and he's using it."

"Painting his house! Why, he only painted it last week, from top to bottom!" said Mrs. Jiffy, amazed. "What in the world is he doing it again for?"

"Well, Jiffy, you must go to Mr. Tock now
and ask him for that ladder of his."

"Er—well," said Jiffy, thinking hard, "somebody horrid came by his house in the night and splashed red and blue paint all over it. It was such a sight that Mr. Tock is going to paint it all again."

"Poor Mr. Tock!" said his mother. "Well, well, well—the things that do happen! I would send you for Dame Goose's ladder, Jiffy, if only it wasn't dinner-time. I do wish we could get Sing-Song's ball for her somehow."

Jiffy was beginning to get very tired of Sing-Song's ball. It was still under the bush. He hoped his mother would forget all about it that afternoon because she was going to a party. Then he could play with the ball and see how high he could throw it and how well it bounced. It certainly was the very finest ball he had ever seen!

Mrs. Jiffy did seem to forget about the ball after dinner. She went to get herself ready for the party. Jiffy wasn't going. He was to stay and look after the house and feed the hens and ducks.

Off went Mrs. Jiffy at three o'clock, looking very nice in her new bonnet. She walked down the lane, and very soon met Mr. Tinky. Jiffy had said that the old man had broken his stick chasing burglars away—but here he was, with his stick, tapping along as usual!

"I suppose he's got it mended already," said Mrs. Jiffy to herself. "Good afternoon, Mr. Tinky. I'm so sorry you had the burglars last

She walked down the lane, and very soon met Mr. Tinky. Jiffy had said that the old man had broken his stick chasing burglars.

night. I hope they didn't take anything."

"Burglars? What burglars?" said old Mr. Tinky, thinking he couldn't have heard properly. "*I* didn't know I had burglars. Nobody told me."

"But, Mr. Tinky—you chased them—you were very brave," said Mrs. Jiffy. "You broke your stick on them!"

"I didn't," said Mr. Tinky. "Here's my stick—and it's not broken, is it? Who told you all that nonsense?"

Mrs. Jiffy didn't answer How very extraordinary! Jiffy had certainly told her about the burglars. She was thinking hard about this when she arrived at Mrs. Doddle's, where the party was to be held. And going in at the gate, whom did she see but Mr. and Mrs. Gobbo!

"Well, Mr. Gobbo! How's your poor back?" she said. Mr. Gobbo stared in surprise.

She stared at Mr Gobbo! Well, well—Jiffy had told her that the poor old fellow had fallen off the step-ladder and hurt his back. She was glad it was better so soon!

"Well, Mr. Gobbo! How's your poor back?" she said kindly. Mr. Gobbo stared in surprise.

"It's all right. Nothing wrong with it as far as I know," he said.

"But—you fell off the step-ladder when it broke," said Mrs. Jiffy.

"What step-ladder? Ours isn't broken," said Mrs. Gobbo. "Some-one's been telling you a tale, Mrs. Jiffy! Mr. Gobbo is as right as rain, and so is our step-ladder!"

Mrs. Jiffy began to feel queer. Jiffy had *certainly* told her all about Mr. Gobbo. How could he have known about it if Mrs. Gobbo hadn't told him? It was very strange. And then she saw Mr. Tock, who was also a guest at the party. She hurried to him.

"Mr. Tock! How tiresome of someone to splash red and blue paint all over your newly painted house! I was so sorry you had to paint it all over again."

Mr. Tock stared at Mrs. Jiffy as if she had gone mad.

"Madam," he said, "no one has splashed red and blue paint over my house as far as I know. And as for painting it all over again, I shouldn't dream of it. What are you talking about?"

"But, Mr. Tock, don't you remember—you used your long ladder to paint your house outside this very morning!" cried Mrs. Jiffy. "Jiffy went to borrow it, and you said he couldn't because you were using it."

Mr. Tock pricked up his ears. So did Mr. and Mrs. Gobbo and Mr. Tinky. "Oho—it was *Jiffy* who told you that, was it?" said Mr. Tock. "Well, we know Jiffy and his great big stories. He's just been telling you fibs, as usual, Mrs. Jiffy—didn't want to do something, I suppose, so he made up all kinds of fairy-tales."

"He didn't come to borrow our step-ladder," said Mrs. Gobbo.

"And he didn't come to borrow my stick," said Mr. Tinky. "But I'll lend it to him, Mrs. Jiffy. I'll certainly lend it to him. You send him along to me this evening, and I'll lend it to him very well indeed!"

Mr. Tock stared at Mrs. Jiffy as if she had gone mad. "Madam," he said, "no one has splashed red and blue paint over my house."

"Ah, yes—you do that," said Mrs. Gobbo.

"I think I *will* send him," said poor Mrs. Jiffy, looking very sad. "He's a naughty boy. He'll have to be stopped or goodness knows what will happen to him. I'll send him along this evening, Mr. Tinky—and you can lend him your stick. Lend it to him hard, won't you?"

And, to Jiffy's great astonishment, when his mother got home after tea she told him he was to go straight off to Mr. Tinky's and borrow his stick.

"It's mended now," said his mother, looking straight at him. "Quite mended. And the burglars have all gone. He can

Hurry up, Jiffy and go. It's your own fault, you know, and I don't feel sorry for you one bit!

use his stick for other bad people again. You go along and ask him to lend it to you."

"Oh, Ma—don't make me!" cried Jiffy in a fright. He didn't like the look on his mother's face at all. "I'll get you the ball—I hid it under the bush. It didn't go in the gutter—and that's why I didn't go and borrow sticks and ladders to get it down. That would have been silly."

"It would," said his mother. "Very silly. I've felt very silly this afternoon, too, saying I was sorry about burglars, and bad backs, and re-painted houses. But now Mr. Tinky *wants* to lend you his stick, so you must go. And I'll get the ball, and you can take it to Sing-Song and say you're sorry when you get back. Go along."

Well, there was nothing for it but to go. Jiffy doesn't want to. He doesn't like Mr. Tinky's stick, and he's going to like it even less now. Hurry up, Jiffy, and go. It's your own fault, you know, and I don't feel sorry for you one bit!

PLACE NAMES FOR YOUR PARTY

WHEN you have your Christmas party why not have a jolly Father Christmas to tell each guest where to sit?

He is very easy to make; all you need is some fairly stiff paper and a few corks.

Trace out the figure shown on this page, transfer it to your card and then, very carefully, cut it out.

Cut about ½″ from one end of a round cork and then cut the piece in half; now make a slit in each piece of cork from the top, or rounded side, almost through to the flat edge. Be careful you don't cut it right through!

The two pieces of cork are Santa's feet. Carefully open each slit and push the base of the figure into it. Now he stands up!

Cut a little strip of paper about ½″ deep and 3½″ wide, write on it the name of your guest and then make a little slit at each end. Bend forward the arms of the figure and push the hands through the two slits in your piece of paper. Now he is holding out the name of your guest!

Make a Father Christmas for each of your friends and colour them with the brightest paints in your box, then your Christmas table will look gayer than ever!

SOMEBODY CAME TO THE DOOR

GEORGE and Anna lived in an old house on the edge of a town. Their father often told them stories about their home.

"My father lived here, and my grandfather," he told them. "And in my grandfather's time it was a farm-house with a big farm round it. But now the town has grown right up to it, and there is no farm—only the house."

"And once our garage held farm-horses," said Anna, who knew all the tales by heart. "And once our sheds were cow-barns and the cows were milked there."

"Yes," said her father, "and your big playroom was the dairy, where the cream was taken off the milk, and where big golden pats of butter were made. It was a lovely cool place then, and fine to see all the bowls of cream set on stone slabs round the walls."

"And now it's our playroom, not a bit cold, and with book-shelves and toy cupboards round instead of stone slabs for cream!" said Anna.

Now one day, when the two children were in their playroom reading, they heard a scrabbling at the door. It was Saturday evening, almost bed-time. Who *could* it be outside? It wasn't the dog, because he was with them, growling at the noise.

Anna went to the door and opened it. At first she could see nobody. Then she felt something running by her foot, and she looked down in surprise. She was more astonished when she saw what the something was!

"George! Look—what is it?" she cried, pointing to a tiny creature running over the playroom floor.

"Gracious!" said George, putting his hand on Tinker's collar. "It's a brownie!"

So it was—a tiny little fellow, no bigger than a small doll. He stood there, looking all round with his bright, bird-like eyes.

"Where's my cream?" he said, in a high voice like a bird's.

"What cream?" said the children, astonished.

"Well, the cream that's always put out for me on Saturday night," said the tiny fellow, stamping his foot. "Get it for me! You know what happens to people who forget to put out my cream for me. I turn their places upside-down!"

"Don't talk like that," said Anna. "We haven't any cream to give you. Why should we, anyway?"

"I always have cream on Saturday night, always!" cried the brownie, with a stamp of his foot again. "The farmer put it down for me in a saucer."

Then suddenly the two children guessed what the tiny creature meant. He was talking about days of long, long ago—when their house was a farm and the room they were in was a dairy!

"Don't you remember, Anna," said George, "Daddy told us how his grandfather used to put down a saucer of cream once a week for the brownie who came for it? If he forgot he would have his bowls of cream

He stood there, looking all round with his bright, bird-like eyes.
"Where's my cream?" he said.

upset and his milk would turn sour!"

"Oh *yes*!" said Anna. She turned to the brownie. "Listen," she said. "You're talking about something that happened ages ago, when this house was a farm in the middle of the country and this playroom was a dairy. We don't keep cows now, we don't have cream, so we certainly can't put any down for you!"

The brownie looked amazed. "Have I been away for long, then?" he said mournfully.

"You must have," said George. "Where have you been since our great-grandfather's time?"

"I was caught by a witch and put to sleep for years," said the

The brownie looked amazed. "Have I been away for long, then?" he said.

brownie. "A hundred years maybe, I don't know. I've only just wakened again, and I came here, where I used to live, for my cream. And I want it, too!"

"What a queer story!" said Anna. "You can't have cream, little man. Listen, here comes our mother. Maybe she will give you milk."

But before Mother came into the room the brownie had vanished. They knew he was somewhere there, though, because Tinker still stared at him. Tinker could often see things they couldn't see. They told their mother all about the tiny man.

She laughed. "You've been reading fairy stories," she said. "There aren't any brownies nowadays. Come along—it's time for bed."

Now the next morning when the children came into their playroom they stopped in horror. What a mess it was in! All the toys had been thrown out of the toy cupboard, the books were scattered on the floor,

But the next morning the room was just as upset!
The children were really cross

the flowers had been taken out of the vase, and their jigsaw puzzles were
upset on the carpet.

"Who's done this?" said Anna. "Oh, George—it must have been that
brownie—just because he didn't get his cream. He's very, very naughty."

"We'll have to catch him," said George. "It's Sunday today, and we'll
be going to church and Sunday school, so we won't have time to plan anything till tomorrow. We'll put everything back and *lock* the cupboard."

But the next morning the room was just as upset! The children were
really cross. "Tinker," they said to their dog, "is the brownie here?
Look at him if he is, because we can't see him now."

Tinker couldn't see him either, so the children knew he wasn't there.
They began to think of some plan to catch and keep him prisoner.

"I know! We could bake some cakes in our toy oven and fill a toy teapot with lemonade and put them on the table in the dolls'-house," said
Anna. "We could leave the door open—and he'd be sure to go in when he
saw the cakes. Then we could lock him in and make him a prisoner!"

"But he'd see us shutting the door," said George.

"We could tie a bit of string to it, pass the string inside the house
and up the chimney—and pull it hard when he's in," said Anna. "Then,
when we pulled, the door would shut, because the string inside the house
would pull it shut when *we* pulled."

"That's a very good idea," said George. So Anna baked some tiny cakes, and George filled the dolls'-house teapot with lemonade. They set out a cup and saucer and plate on the kitchen table inside the dolls'-house.

Then they tied black thread to the inside handle of the front door, ran it through the kitchen and up the chimney till it came out at the top. They ran the thread right to the toy cupboard.

"We'll both hide in the big toy cupboard," said George. "Then as soon as the brownie comes in and goes to the house we'll pull the string—and click, the door will shut and he'll be caught! We can rush to the house and lock the door with its tiny key. He can't get out of the windows because they don't open!"

"How shall we know when he goes into the house? We hardly ever *see* him," said Anna. "He's nearly always invisible."

"Well, we'll *shut* the little front door," said George, "and we shall see it opening when he goes inside. We shall know then."

That night they hid in the toy cupboard, leaving the door open just a

They **tied black** thread to the inside handle of the front door, ran it through the kitchen and up the chimney till it came out at the top.

crack so that they could see. After a while they thought they heard pattering footsteps on the floor. Then they felt sure the brownie was reading the little note they had left for him. George had written it.

"Please don't upset our playroom again. Go into the dolls'-house, where you will find we have set a meal ready for you."

The note went up in the air and down, as if someone had picked it up, read it, and put it down again. And then they saw the door of the dolls'-house opening! The brownie was going inside!

Quick as lightning George pulled hard at the black thread that ran across the floor, up the side of the dolls'-house, down the chimney and over to the inside handle of the little front door. It shut with a click! "Hold it shut with the string, Anna, whilst I go and lock it!" cried George.

What a to-do there was when the brownie found himself a prisoner! How he squealed and kicked and stamped! How he threw things about in the dolls'-house! It was really dreadful. He was a very naughty little thing indeed.

That night they hid in the toy cupboard, leaving the door open just a crack so that they could see.

He made himself visible at once and they saw him peering out of one of the windows.
"Let me out, let me out!" he yelled.

He made himself visible at once and they saw him peering out of one of the windows. "Let me out, let me out!" he yelled. But they didn't. That was last week, and he's still there! What in the world are they to do with him?

They asked their old Granny, because their mother and father wouldn't believe them. She laughed—but she told them what to do.

"You take him in the dolls'-house to the nearest farm you know," she said. "One that has a dairy with cream! Set him free there, and he'll never come back to plague you."

So that's what they are going to do. I hope the farmer's wife puts down a little cream for him each week, don't you? It isn't often that a farmhouse has its own brownie these days.

AT THE BUS STOP

Quite a lot of people were standing at the bus-stop. Denis and Valerie were there, of course, because they always caught the bus back home from school at that time. John was there, too, a boy in their class, and Eileen, who was in the class above.

There were two men and two women as well, talking together. "The bus is late," said one. "I wish it would hurry up. I want to get home."

Denis and Valerie wanted to get home, too. It was exams the next day and they wanted to read their notes over and over so that they would do good geography and history papers. Bother the bus!

There suddenly came a little tinkling noise, and one of the women gave a cry. 'Oh! My bracelet has slipped off my wrist! Where is it?"

Everyone looked down to see. But it wasn't there. The woman pointed to a drain just beside the kerb. "It went down there. Look—you can just see it between the bars of the grating! Can one of you lift up the grating and get it for me?"

But nobody could. It seemed to be fastened down so that it couldn't be lifted. The woman bent down and tried to slip her hand through the grating.

"My hand's too big," she said. "I wonder—would one of these children have a small enough hand to slip through and get my bracelet? It's such a valuable one."

"The bus is coming," said John. "I can't stop to try. Come on, Eileen. You'll miss the bus if you try to get the bracelet."

John, Eileen and one of the men and the other woman all got on the bus. It rumbled off, leaving Valerie, Denis, the woman who had lost her bracelet and the man who was with her. The woman was almost crying now.

"It was the lovely bracelet you gave me when you married me," she said to the man. "Oh, *can't* we get it?"

Denis had stayed behind to see if he could manage to get the brace-let for the woman. It was a nuisance to miss the bus, but, after all, you had to help if you could.

"I'll try," he said, and knelt down. But his hand was *just* too big.

"*I'll* try," said Valerie, though she hated the idea of putting her hand down into the dirty, smelly drain. Oooh, how horrid!

But her small hand slid through easily and her fingers groped for the bracelet. They touched it. She got it between her two longest fingers, and carefully edged her hand back through the grating. Denis bent over and caught the bracelet as soon as it appeared above the grating. He held it up to the delighted woman.

"Oh, *thank* you! That's marvel-lous! What's your name? I must give you a reward."

"No, that's all right," said Denis and Valerie together, and they ran off down the road, because they knew that they could get home be-

Denis had stayed behind to see if he could manage to get the bracelet.

fore the next bus came—there was such a long wait in between the buses in the late afternoon.

The two children felt pleased when they got home. It was nice to know they had got back the bracelet. Mother was pleased about it, too.

But when Denis got out his notes to revise them after tea he didn't feel at all pleased. He had lost his precious fountain-pen!

He felt in all his pockets. Then he smacked his hand crossly on the table. "Valerie! It must have slipped out when I was kneeling down over that grating! I *thought* I felt something sliding by my knee, but I was so taken up with the bracelet I didn't look to see."

"Oh, Denis! We got the bracelet, but we lost your pen! And it's exams tomorrow!" said Valerie. "We didn't deserve to lose your pen. I'd lend you mine for the exams, but its nib has gone all crooked and it's simply dreadful to write with now. Oh dear—now you'll have to use an ordinary pen and keep dipping it in the ink-pot. That *will* put you off your exams!"

He had lost his precious fountain-pen!
He felt in all his pockets.

"We'll look for the pen when we get out of the bus to-morrow," said Denis gloomily. "But someone will be sure to have seen it and picked it up."

It wasn't there, of course. Denis went to school feeling very mournful—his nice pen lost—and just as exams were on, too—and poor Valerie's pen wasn't much use, either. It wasn't any good borrowing that.

After prayers that morning, just as the children turned to march out, the headmaster held up his hand.

"One moment," he said. "I have a letter here. It concerns two children from this school

Denis and Valerie stood out, blushing fiery red. Good gracious!
Fancy anyone writing a letter about them!

who missed the bus yesterday through doing someone a kindness—getting a valuable bracelet from a drain. They wouldn't give their names
or take a reward. Who were those two children, please?"

Denis and Valerie stood out, blushing fiery red. Good gracious!
Fancy anyone writing a letter about them!

The headmaster smiled at them. "Thank you for bringing credit on the
school," he said. "With the letter was a parcel for you. Here it is."

Denis took it, and when he opened it—guess what was inside! Yes,
you're right—two smart little fountain-pens, one for him and one for
Valerie! What a bit of luck!

"*I expect you've both got fine fountain-pens*," said the note with the presents.
"*But you never know when they might get broken or be lost—so here are two, just
in case!*"

You should have seen the children's faces! "It's like magic!" said
Valerie, beaming. "*Now* we shall be able to write some fine exam papers!"

They did, of course—and they were top. Their mother was very
pleased, indeed—and so am I. It's just the sort of thing that *should* happen,
isn't it?

THEY WOULDN'T BE FRIENDS WITH HIM

PRINCE KIRRION felt very pleased with himself   He meant to run away for the whole afternoon and have a good time—and it looked as if he would be able to do exactly what he had planned.

He was lying in bed. The curtains were pulled across the windows to keep out the bright afternoon sun. His governess had tiptoed out of the room after telling him she wouldn't disturb him till five o'clock.

"Poor little prince!" she said. "Such a nasty thing to have a bad headache. You must have been out in the sun too much. You were a good boy to tell me so that I could pop you into bed to get you better."

Prince Kirrion grinned to himself when he thought of all she had said. As soon as the door was safely shut he leaned on his elbow and looked round the room. There were his clothes put neatly on a chair—but he wasn't going to wear those. No—he had a suit of clothes hidden safely away in a drawer, a suit that he had taken out of someone else's room. It belonged to one of the king's pages.

Kirrion was eleven years old, and he thought the world of himself. His mother thought the world of him, too. His father didn't see him very often because he was king and had a great deal to do. He was pleased, though, that Kirrion was good-looking, strong and clever.

Kirrion was bored with life in the palace He didn't like Dame Rosalind, his governess, and he disliked his tutor, too.

"He shouldn't make me work so hard!" thought Kirrion sulkily "As if it matters whether a king knows how to spell properly or not! He's always got somebody to do his spelling for him, hasn't he? It's a waste of my time to bother about spelling and tables. I want to go out into the world and do the things other boys and girls do."

He often thought of the other children he saw from his carriage when he went riding. Sometimes the boys were fishing in the stream. Sometimes they were picnicking by the field-side. Often they were playing cricket or football on the greens. They shouted and laughed and chased one another. Kirrion wanted to do all that, too.

And now he was really going to! He had got this suit of clothes by a very clever trick, and he had told Dame Rosalind that he had a bad headache and wanted to rest till it went. Now he was going to dress himself in the suit of clothes, steal downstairs to the larder and take some food, then slip out by the garden gate to find someone to go picnicking with.

"I'm very clever," thought Prince Kirrion. "Nobody dreams how clever I am! Whilst they all think I'm lying here with a headache I shall be out in the countryside with a basket of food, making all kinds of new friends. How proud people will be to be friends with a prince!"

It was a hot spring day. Kirrion got out of bed and listened. No one was about. Most people were in their rooms, resting after a long meeting in the council hall that morning. It was just the time to slip out now.

Kirrion dressed in the suit of clothes he had taken from the little page's chest of drawers. It was the boy's home suit, a plain brown tunic and short knickerbockers, with long stockings and brown leather sandals. Kirrion thought he looked very ordinary and plain in them. He was used to wearing very grand clothes indeed.

Kirrion dressed in the suit of clothes he had taken from the little page's chest of drawers. It was the boy's home suit.

He slipped out of his room and ran quietly to the back stairs. He went down them cautiously. He stood at the bottom and listened. Most of the servants had gone to watch the first cricket match of the season on the nearby green. One or two were still left, and Kirrion could hear them talking in the big pantry.

There was no one in the kitchen. He slipped in and ran to the larder. In a trice he had stuffed all kinds of things into a big basket. What a fine picnic he would have with whatever new friends he found!

Then out he went into the garden and down to the old gate in the wall. He was soon standing in the lane, full of delight. Now his adventure was beginning!

He made his way into the nearby wood. He had meant to walk for miles right away from the palace, but he soon felt tired. He wished he could meet some other children. Where could they have gone to this afternoon?

He sat down to rest under a tree. All round him were big clumps of yellow primroses. It was a nice place to rest in.

A little dog came running up to him, panting. It licked his face, and Kirrion was cross. "Get away, I tell you, or I'll throw a stone at you!"

"Don't you dare!" said a girl's voice, and a little girl of about Kirrion's age came round a tree. "All dogs lick. What's the harm in that?"

There was no one in the kitchen. He slipped in and ran to the larder.
In a trice he had stuffed all kinds of things into a big basket.

120

Then a boy came along, too. He was a bit older than Kirrion. The little prince was pleased to see them both, though he felt cross at being spoken to so sharply by the girl.

"What are you doing in the wood?" asked Kirrion, remembering to be polite.

"Picking primroses for Mother," said the little girl. "We haven't any in our garden at all."

"Well, let's dig some up, then," said Kirrion at once. "Oh—there's nothing to dig with. Well, let's pull up some roots, then." He tugged at a big primrose clump and up it came.

"Don't do that," said the little girl, shocked. "People can

He tugged at a big primrose clump and up it came. "Don't do that," said the girl.

pick flowers in woods, but it's wrong to dig up the whole plant. Why, if everyone did that there would soon be no flowers left to pick."

"Pooh! Take what you want," said Kirrion. "That's what I always do." He tugged at another primrose root. The little girl stopped him. "Don't, please. We shan't take them home, because our mother wouldn't like us to steal them from the wood."

Kirrion tugged harder. The boy spoke; his voice was so commanding that Kirrion obeyed. "Leave the primroses alone! Do you hear?"

The prince felt nervous. Nobody ever spoke to him like that! He remembered his picnic basket. The children would be friends with him if he shared his food with them. He pulled everything out of the basket.

"Come and picnic with me," he begged them. "Look—here's a whole roast chicken—and look at this lovely pie! And did you ever see such nice jam-tarts? There's this cream-cake, too. Let's all share."

The boy and girl looked in amazement at the rich food.

He quite expected the children to kneel down before him and beg his pardon.
But they didn't. They laughed scornfully.

"Where did you get that from?" asked the boy. "Why, that's food fit for a king!"

That made Kirrion laugh heartily. "That's a good joke!" he said. "It was meant to be food for a king—the king himself! I crept into the palace larder and took it for a picnic meal. What do you think of that?"

"I think you're a dreadful story-teller," said the little girl. "Really dreadful. I'm quite sure you've never been inside the palace! And if you did take that food from the larder, you're a thief!"

"You're a nasty girl," said Kirrion angrily. "And I'll just tell you this: I'm the prince of this country—Prince Kirrion!"

He quite expected the children to kneel down before him and beg his pardon. But they didn't. They laughed scornfully.

"Story-teller!" said the girl. "Silly, stupid story-teller!"

"I tell you it's true," said Kirrion, red with rage. "Why shouldn't it be? Is it because I've got on plain brown clothes? Well, I took those out of a drawer in one of the pages' rooms. He didn't know anything about it. I was too clever! I expect he got into trouble for losing it."

"Why do you make yourself out to be so horrid?" said the boy. "Do you really think these things are clever?"

"I'm not horrid!" cried Kirrion, and he leapt to his feet. "Look here —I'm the prince himself. I told my silly old governess I'd got a headache and wanted to go to bed. But as soon as she left me I got into these clothes, took this food out of the larder, and came into these woods to find some children for friends, to share a picnic with me. Why don't you believe me? Don't I *look* like a prince?"

"No," said the little girl. "You've got a mean face, for one thing. And you tell stories and steal things, for another. Princes don't behave like that. The king of this country is a fine man. I've often heard my father say so. He wouldn't have a son like you, I'm sure. You're just a fraud."

The little prince was so angry that he could hardly think of a word to say. He roared with rage and stamped around among the prim-roses. The other two watched him and laughed. He couldn't bear that.

He picked up the roast chicken and threw it at the little girl. He threw the meat-pie at the boy.

In a trice he felt two strong hands on his arms. He felt a hard slap on his face. He found himself on his back, with somebody tying up his hands.

It was the boy. "I'll show you what happens to kids who hurt my sister!" the boy was saying fiercely. "You'll be tied up to this tree till you say you're sorry, you mean, bad-tempered, boastful little fellow!"

With tears of rage pouring down his cheeks, Kirrion was soon tied to a small tree. The boy and the girl stood looking at him. "Prince,

In a trice he felt two strong hands on his arms. He felt a hard slap on his face.

123

indeed!" said the boy scornfully. "More likely you're the son of somebody put in prison for doing bad things. That's where you'll be put, too, one of these days! Now, just you say you're sorry!"

"I shan't say I'm sorry, I shan't, I shan't!" wept Kirrion, struggling to get free. "I'll stay here for weeks and weeks before I say I'm sorry. You've insulted the prince. You'll both be whipped for this!"

"Come on. Let's leave him there," said the boy. "We'll come back after tea and see if he's learnt any sense."

So they left him and went home. They had their tea, and went back to the wood where they had left Kirrion. But on the way they heard the sound of horses' hoofs. Along came a big man on horseback, followed by six others. They reined in their horses when they saw the two children.

"Have you seen a boy in prince's clothing?" the first horseman asked.

"No," said the little girl. "We met a stupid boy in the woods who said he was the prince, but he wasn't. He was very rude and silly, and we tied him up."

"Tell me about it," said the horseman. The boy told him all that had happened.

"He actually dared to say he was the *prince*," he finished. "But no prince would behave like that, so we didn't believe him. And when he

Along came a big man on horseback, followed by six others. "Have you seen a boy in prince's clothing?" the first horseman asked.

"I'll just keep behind a tree," he said. "I want to see this bad boy.
You go and talk to him."

threw things at my little sister and hurt her I slapped him, knocked him
down and tied him up. We're just on our way to him now. If he says he's
sorry we'll let him go."

"Just fancy! He wanted us to be friends with him and have a picnic,"
said the little girl. "As if we would be friends with a boy like that!"

"I'll come with you," said the horseman, and he signed to the other
riders to stop where they were. He leapt off his horse, left it and went
with the children.

"I'll just keep behind a tree," he said. "I want to see this bad boy.
You go and talk to him."

The two children were puzzled by the big horseman. What had happened? Why was he looking for a boy dressed in prince's clothing?
Surely he couldn't be looking for that silly boy they had tied up?

They came to the tree where they had tied up the prince. He was crying
with fright. "Let me go, let me go! I'm sorry! I won't do it again. I'm
frightened of being here alone. Let me go!"

"Are you sorry you pulled up the primroses by their roots?" demanded the little girl. "Are you sorry you told such stories? Are you sorry you threw things at us, and lost your temper?"

"Yes, I'm sorry, I'm sorry," wept Kirrion. "But I didn't tell you stories. I *am* the prince. I did give my governess the slip. I did take those things out of the larder, and I did take this suit from one of the pages at the palace."

"Silly!" said the little girl. The boy went to untie the prince from the tree. As soon as he was free Kirrion turned on them.

"You horrid children! You think you can do these things to me, the prince! I'll show you what happens to people who do that to me! I'll have you whipped! I'll have you locked up with nothing but bread and water. I'll . . . I'll . . ."

"Kirrion," said a stern voice, and from behind the tree stepped the big horseman. Kirrion knew him at once and trembled.

"Your Majesty, my father!" he whispered.

"Kirrion," said a stern voice, and from behind the tree stepped the big horseman. Kirrion knew him at once and trembled.

"It all began that day I ran into the woods," he said. "What a good thing you two laughed at me and tied me up."

The other two children went pale and knelt down before the king.

"Get up," said the king. "It is my son who should kneel to us, not you to me. Little did I think that I would find in two strange children all the good things that are missing in my own son! Kirrion, you shall have the punishment you planned to give to these two children. You will be whipped and locked up for two days on bread and water."

"Oh, don't whip him," said the little girl. "He's so frightened now."

"So you are kind as well as good!" said the king. "What a pity my son hasn't friends like you!"

"I want them for my friends," wept the prince. "I like them. My father, Your Majesty, may they be friends and come to the palace?"

"We will see," said the king, and took Kirrion away.

"I hope we shall never see the king again," said the little girl to her brother that night. "He might be angry with us next time."

But they did see him again, many times, and they grew to love him. He sent for them to play with Kirrion, and to have lessons with him.

"You can teach him far more than any governess or tutor!" he told them. "Do your best!" It was a very good best. Kirrion grew up into a king as fine as his father—but he has never forgotten how it happened.

"It all began that day I ran into the woods," he said. "What a good thing you two laughed at me and tied me up."

And I really think it was.

THE PIXIE'S WEDDING

In Cuckoo Wood there's a wedding today,
  And the pixies are there in a grand array
To see the marriage of Hoppetty Ho
  With the pretty young pixie, Tippetty-Toe.
The bluebells will ring out a wedding chime,
  The nightingales promised to sing all the time,
The hawthorn is throwing confetti around
  And spreading a carpet of white on the ground.
Hoppetty's cloak is of poppies red,
  Tippetty's veil is of spider's thread.
When they're married they'll live in a toadstool
      house,
  And to keep it clean they've a little brown
      mouse.
They've asked me to visit them some time soon,
  So I'm going on Midsummer's Night in June!

128

*The sea-lions bark a loud welcome when the
keeper comes along with fish for their dinner!
They are very clever at catching it, and never miss.*

DICKY DAWDLE'S ADVENTURES

ICKY DAWDLE was just like his name. He was a real dawdler! He dawdled over his dressing in the morning, so that he was always late for breakfast. He was slow over his porridge, so that he was always late for school. He dreamed over his lessons, so he nearly always missed his playtime!

One day he met a little pixie fellow ambling down the lane, his hands in his pockets and his coat buttoned up wrong.

"Hello," said Dicky in surprise, for he saw that the little fellow was a pixie. "Who are you?"

"My name's Dickory Dawdle," said the little fellow.

"How funny!" said Dicky. "Mine's Dicky Dawdle. Where do you live?"

"In Pixie Wood," said Dickory. "I say, come along and spend the night with me, and I'll take you to the Brownie's Circus tomorrow. It's very, very good. You'll love it! And if there's time we'll go to the Wise Gnome's party!"

"Oooh!" said Dicky, excited. "I'll go and ask my mother."

His mother said yes, he might go. So Dicky packed his night-clothes and his tooth-brush and sponge and went to find Dickory again.

Together they went down the lane, through a hole in the hedge, over a stile that Dicky had never seen before—and there they were in Pixie Wood! It was a most exciting place, for fairies, pixies and gnomes trotted

What games the tiger cubs have in the big cage where they live with their mother and father! Do you see the mother licking one cub just as if he were a kitten?

He would get the cloth to lay the table, and then put it down on a chair to do
something else and forget all about the cloth.

about everywhere, going marketing, chatting to one another, and popping
in and out of tree-houses and toadstool cottages.

"We'll go to bed early, Dicky," said Dickory. "You see, we must
catch the eight-o'clock bus if we want to get to High-Up Hill, where
the circus is held, in good time to buy front seats."

It was all very fine Dickory saying that—but he took such a long
time getting the supper that Dicky was half asleep before it was finished!

Dickory Dawdle had a nice little house in a tree, with two round
rooms—a sitting-room and a bedroom, one above the other. He *was* a
dawdler! He would get the cloth to lay the table, and then put it down
on a chair to do something else and forget all about the cloth.

Then he would spend half an hour hunting in the drawer again to find
the cloth. Dicky got quite cross with him.

Supper was lovely. It was chocolate pudding with ice-cream sauce,
and ginger-beer to drink through long straws. But Dickory Dawdle was so
long serving out the pudding that the ice-cream sauce melted into custard!

They finished their supper at last, and Dickory Dawdle got up to clear away. But he dawdled about so much that the table was still uncleared in half an hour's time, and Dicky began to do it himself. He was so sleepy by this time that he longed to go to bed.

"Do hurry up, Dickory," he said. "I never knew anyone so slow as you!"

"Oh yes, you know some one *just* as slow," said Dickory crossly. "*You* are a real dawdler, too. I knew it as soon as I saw you mooning along the lane, just looking at nothing! I wouldn't have asked you to spend the night with me if I'd thought you were going to be impatient. Go to bed if you want to!"

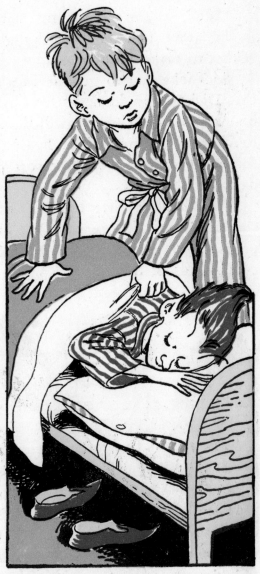

So Dicky undressed and got into the tiny bed that Dickory showed him. Dickory spent such a long time finding his pyjamas and dawdling round the room that Dicky was asleep long before Dickory was even in bed!

Dicky had a watch. He looked at it when he woke up. He didn't want to miss the bus that went to High-Up Hill, for he badly wanted to see the Brownies' Circus.

"Hie, Dickory, it's seven o'clock already!" said Dicky. He jumped out of bed. This was a marvellous thing for him to do without being told, for he was usually very lazy indeed in the mornings!

Dickory didn't stir. Dicky pushed and shook him. "Leave me alone," said Dickory. "There's plenty of time."

Dickory didn't stir. Dicky pushed and shook him. "Leave me alone," said Dickory.

"Well, we've got to dress and have breakfast," said Dicky impatiently. "I'll pull you out of bed!"

He did—and then Dickory *had* to get up, though he was very sulky about it. And, dear me, *how* he dawdled! He put a sock on—and then he sat on the bed and dreamed for a while. Then he put on another sock. After that he wandered round the room, whistling. Dicky watched him, feeling cross.

"Do hurry, Dickory. I want some breakfast before we go."

"Well, set the table then," said Dickory. "There is some cold ham in the larder, and we'll have ginger-beer to drink again. It's too much bother to make tea or cocoa."

So Dicky had to get the breakfast, because he could quite well see that Dickory would never have time.

And then Dickory dawdled over breakfast! He took ten minutes to chew one mouthful of ham! Dicky got crosser and crosser, quite forgetting that this was the sort of thing he usually did himself every day.

They left the dirty breakfast-things on the table and went to catch the bus. But Dickory wouldn't hurry a bit. He said there was plenty of time. He put his hands in his pockets and dawdled along, thinking of all kinds of things.

He put a sock on—and then he sat on the bed and dreamed for a while. Then he put on another sock.

And when they got to the bus stop, in the middle of the wood, the bus was gone! There it was in the distance, a dear little yellow bus full of fairies and elves going to the circus! Dicky could have cried with rage.

"It's all your silly fault!" he said to Dickory. "If you hadn't been so slow over everything we would easily have caught the bus."

"Well, you're a fine fellow to talk, I must say!" said Dickory in surprise. "I've always heard that you are very slow yourself. Didn't I hear that you were late for school every day last week?"

Dicky went red. It was quite

There were apples and custard, but as Dickory forgot to watch the custard cooking it burnt.

true. He and Dickory went back to the tree-house without saying a word more. They washed up, and then Dicky asked about the Gnome's party.

"What time have we to be there?" he said.

"Half-past two," said Dickory. "Heaps of time. We'll have dinner at twelve, and a little snooze afterwards."

"A snooze!" said Dicky. "I don't want a snooze!"

"Oh yes you do," said Dickory firmly. "All dawdlers like forty winks and snoozes and naps. Now don't start shouting at me or hurrying me, because I just won't have it. I'm a dawdler, like you, and I WON'T BE HURRIED!"

Well, they didn't have dinner at twelve, because Dickory dawdled so much over the potatoes that they were not cooked till one. There were stewed apples and custard, too, and cold chicken, but as Dickory forgot to watch the custard cooking it got burnt and he had to make some more. So it was about one o'clock when they sat down to dinner.

And though Dicky ate quickly, with his eyes on the cuckoo-clock that hung on the wall, Dickory would *not* hurry himself. He dawdled over his chicken, he dawdled over his pudding. Dicky was nearly in despair.

"We shall be late for the party!" he said.

"Plenty of time, plenty of time," said Dickory, yawning. "We *must* have a snooze first." And the tiresome little fellow lay down on the couch and went straight off to sleep.

At a quarter-past two there was a knock on the tree-door. As Dickory was asleep, Dicky opened the door. There was a small fairy outside, very smartly dressed, all ready for the party. She smiled at Dicky.

"The rabbit carriage is here to take you and Dickory to the party," she said. "We are all waiting for you."

"Dickory's asleep!" cried Dicky, and he ran to shake the pixie. The fairy looked upset.

"We can't wait whilst you wash and tidy yourselves," she said. "And you can't possibly come like that. Look at your coat, Dickory! You've

Dicky opened the door. There was a small fairy outside, very smartly dressed, all ready for the party.

134

spilt custard all down it! You're such a dawdler that it would take you ages to change it. We shan't wait for you. Good-bye!"

"Oh, but can't you take me without Dickory?" asked Dicky, disappointed.

"Oh no!" said the fairy. "Come another time, but don't get Dawdle to take you or you'll never get there!"

She ran off. Dicky was very angry with Dickory. He put on his cap and went to the door.

"I'm going home," he said. "I'll never get anywhere if I leave things to you. You dreadful slowcoach!"

"Now just stop calling me names!" said Dickory angrily

You should have seen Dicky jump out of bed! You should have seen him run to school!

as he at last rose slowly from the couch. "Who's a slow old snail and never finishes his dinner till it's time for afternoon school? *You* are! Who's as slow as a tortoise over going to bed each night? *You* are!"

But Dicky wouldn't listen to any more. It was dreadful to hear things like that—because he knew they were true.

"Well, if that's what it's like living with a dawdler, no wonder Mummy gets angry with *me*," said Dicky as he hurried home. "It seems as if dawdlers miss all the good things and all the treats. My word, Mummy's going to get a surprise tomorrow!"

And she did! You should have seen how Dicky jumped out of bed when he was called! You should have seen him run to school! And before the morning had gone he was top of the class.

Do you dawdle? Well, go and spend a day with Dickory Dawdle and tell me how you like it!

TWO PUZZLES

1

I'm a poor lost cat—behead me, please,
And I'll carry your breakfasts, dinners
and teas.
Behead me again and I'll light your way;
Once more behead me—I'm half of a bray!

Find the four words.

2

Every day to the well I go,
Change my head—on your thumb
I grow!
Change my head once more, and then
I'll grow on dog, cat, horse or hen!

Answers on page 174.

HEE-HAW

THE PRISONER IN THE CAVE

"Let's go and play in the wood on Windy Hill," said Michael. "It's a lovely sunny day, and there won't be many more chances this autumn of going there."

"All right," said Janet. "I'd like that. We might see if any squirrels are about. We may see them collecting nuts and acorns."

So off they went. The woods were lovely. The children wandered through the trees, and then saw a red squirrel. A *red* one! How lovely. They had only seen grey ones before.

"Quick! Let's follow it," said Michael, so they tracked it through the woods. It bounded lightly along the boughs of the trees, then down to the ground to pick up an acorn.

"We might see where it has its hidey-hole," said Janet softly. Isn't it lovely! I do like the way it sits up, don't you?"

"Oh—it's gone," said Michael. "It rushed up that tree and into the next, and it's gone. We must have frightened it."

Janet looked round and about. "Where exactly are we?" she said. "I've never been on this part of the hill before. Oh, Michael, do you think we're near the hill-caves? We have never been able to find them, you know."

"We'll look round a bit and see," said Michael. "I know they're some-where half-way up the hill, and that's about where we are."

They wandered round a bit, and then Janet called out in excitement: "Look! There's a cave, surely? That dark patch over there."

They ran to where Janet was pointing. Yes, it *was* a cave! How exciting!

"Shall we go in?" said Janet. "It looks a bit dark and gloomy."

"Of course we'll go in," said Michael. "We must explore! Caves are fun—you never know what you'll find in them or where they lead to, or where they end. Think of all the thousands and thousands of caves under the earth that nobody has ever been in—how I'd like to explore them all!"

They peeped in at the cave entrance. It was certainly dark in the cave. "Have you got a torch?" asked Janet. "I'm not going in unless you have."

"Yes, I've got one," said Michael. "It's the one I had for my birthday last week. Come on."

He switched on his torch and the beam lighted up the cave at once. It was narrow and rather long. It smelt a bit damp and musty, and Janet didn't like it very much.

He switched on his torch and the beam lighted up the cave at once.
It was narrow and rather long.

138

"Let's play we've been ship-wrecked and found a cave to shelter in," said Michael. "We'll make it our home. Go and get some dry bracken and we'll make a bed. There's a kind of shelf here at the side of the cave that will do beauti-fully for one."

Janet went to get some bracken. Soon the two children had made a very fine bed to lie on. "Now we really ought to make a fire at the cave entrance to keep away wild animals," said Michael.

But they couldn't do that because neither of them had any matches. So they put a little pile of sticks at the entrance, pretending that it really was alight.

"I've found a tiny stream run-ning down the hill just nearby," said Janet, coming back with some more bracken. "That's lucky for us. We shall have water to drink whilst we're shipwrecked."

"What about food?" asked Michael. "I suppose we could eat nuts and things, like the squirrels. There might be a few blackberries, too."

They put a little pile of sticks at the entrance and pretended that it was a fire.

They managed to find a few late blackberries, rather squashy and small, and they picked up some acorns.

"Not much food for two poor shipwrecked sailors!" said Janet solemnly, as she put them down on a tiny ledge above their "bed".

"Now let's play being shipwrecked right from the beginning," said Michael. "We stagger up the hill, moaning—we find the cave and stumble into it gladly—we fall on our bed and sleep for hours. Let's do that."

Then she fell back, pretending to be asleep. Michael did the same. For a minute
or two there was complete silence in the cave.

So, much to the surprise of two rabbits who were watching from under
a bush, the two children came staggering up the hillside, giving strange
moans. Janet even stopped to pretend to wring water out of her clothes.
"Wet and cold!" she kept saying. "Shipwrecked and almost drowned."

"Nobody saved but us," said Michael, wringing water out of his jersey.

"Look—a cave!" said Janet, so suddenly that she made Michael jump.
"We must rest. I can go no farther."

"It may be a cave for wild animals," said Michael. "Perhaps they sleep
there at night."

"Then we will build a fire to keep them away," said Janet, who was
really very good at pretending.

They stumbled into the cave and flung themselves down on the bed of
bracken at the side. Janet gave some realistic groans. Then she fell
back, pretending to be asleep. Michael did the same. For a minute or
two there was complete silence in the cave.

And then something very surprising happened. Footsteps came up to
the cave and somebody peeped in. The children heard the steps and sat up.

"Hist!" said Michael in Janet's ear. "Savages! Don't move!"

At the cave entrance stood a man. He was bare-headed, but they could
not see his face. He carried something in his hands. It looked like a bag
of some sort—a paper bag.

He came right into the cave, switching on a torch as he did so. He did not swing the beam of light to the side of the cave, but straight in front of him. So he didn't catch sight of the silent children sitting up on their bed of bracken. To their intense surprise he walked right to the back of the cave—and then disappeared!

They heard faint sounds in the distance. Where had the man gone? Was there another cave right at the back—or a passage or something?

Michael clutched Janet and whispered again. "What's he doing back there? Does he live here, do you suppose?"

"Oh dear—if he's a tramp who lives in these caves he won't be very pleased at finding us here," said Janet. "Let's go."

But before they could go they heard sounds again, and the man came back. He carried something else in his hands now. Michael strained his eyes to see what it was. It was a big jug!

"A jug!" he thought. "He must be going to get some water. So he does live here! I bet he's going to that little stream."

Before they could go they heard sounds again, and the man came back. He carried something else in his hands now. It was a big jug!

141

The man went out of the cave. The children did not like to escape just then in case the man saw them, because the stream was only just nearby. So they covered themselves with the bracken and lay quite still, waiting for him to come back. Janet's heart was beating rather fast. It all seemed rather queer somehow.

The man came back almost at once, carrying the jug carefully as if it were full of water. He disappeared at the back of the cave again.

"He *must* live here," said Michael. "He's taken food and drink to some cave at the back that he has made into his home."

"Well, let's go, then," said Janet. "It's getting dark."

But before they could go the man came back again, without the jug, and walked straight out of the cave and down the hill.

"Why—he's gone," said Michael, puzzled. "Where's he gone? Why doesn't he stay in his cave now it's getting dark?"

"Michael—listen—what's that noise?" suddenly said Janet, clutching at Michael's arm. They both listened. A curious, faraway noise came from the back of the cave. What was it? A moan—a groan—a howl? And who was making it, back there in the heart of the hill?

"Oh, Michael—there's a prisoner in the cave behind this one," said Janet, frightened. "There is, there is! And it's he who is making that awful noise."

The man came back almost at once, carrying the jug carefully as if it were full of water. He disappeared at the back of the cave.

"It does seem queer," said Michael, not liking it at all. "It really looks as if there must be somebody who is being kept prisoner—the man certainly took food and drink there."

"Probably he comes every day to bring some," said Janet. "Goodness—it's all very strange. What shall we do?"

"Do you think we'd better see if we can find the prisoner?" asked Michael, who wasn't really feeling very brave at the moment.

"Oh, I'd be scared to," said Janet. "But I suppose we *ought* to try and rescue him. Shall we—shall we just go to the back of the cave and see where it leads?"

"All right," said Michael, switching on his torch. "But

They turned and fled. They didn't stop running till they were half-way down the hill!

we'd better hurry, because it will be dark soon!"

They went on tiptoe to the back of the cave. At first they could see nothing but rocky wall—then Michael's torch picked out a small opening.

"Look—that's where the man went through. I bet there's a passage there, leading to somewhere else."

A strange sound came booming up from behind the cave they were in. That was enough for the two children. They turned and fled, trampling down the twigs they had arranged for their fire. They didn't stop running till they were half-way down the hill!

"Oh dear—what dreadful cowards we are," said Janet, panting, "to leave that poor prisoner behind, moaning like that. Well, it's so dark I simply daren't go back. We'd better go home and talk about it."

So they went down the hill and soon came to the town they lived in. As they passed the bus-stop a bus came up and a man got on to it. Janet pulled at Michael's arm.

"Look—isn't that the bare-headed man we saw in our cave? Yes—it is. He's catching the bus, so he *doesn't* live in the cave. There *is* a prisoner there that he takes food and water to!"

The children went home. They would tell their mother. She would know what to do. But she was out. What a pity! "Well, let's pop in next door and tell Harry and Mark," said Michael. "They'll be thrilled."

They were! In fact they were so thrilled that they wanted to solve the mystery themselves and not tell any grown-up.

"Don't tell your mother," begged Harry. "Let's all go up there tomorrow afternoon and find out where the prisoner is and what his name is, and why he's being kept in the cave. This is all very exciting, you know. How lucky you were to go to those caves this afternoon!"

So it was decided that the secret should be kept, and the next day all four should go up to the hill-cave and explore thoroughly what lay behind it. They would rescue the prisoner by themselves!

They were so thrilled that they wanted to solve the mystery themselves.

"I don't believe tomorrow will *ever* come!" said Janet that night. But it did, of course—and brought a very exciting day with it!

The next afternoon Michael, Janet, Harry and Mark met outside in the road. Each of them had a torch with a new battery in it. Nobody was going to risk being in the dark!

"Isn't this exciting!" said Janet, who felt very brave now that she and Michael had two big boys with them. "What shall we find, I wonder? Shall we see that man again—the one who took in food and water?"

"Not if he comes at the same time as he did yesterday," said Michael, looking at his watch.

Soon they came to the cave opening. They stood and looked at it. The entrance
was dark and quiet. Not a sound was to be heard.

"We're too early to see him if he comes at the same time. As we think
we saw him going off by bus yesterday evening it's likely he *comes* here by
bus, too—and probably catches the same one each time."

"We'll be able to explore without being afraid he'll pounce on us,
then," said Janet thankfully. "This way, Harry—up between these trees—
and then to the left. Yesterday was the first time we'd been this way."

Soon they came to the cave opening. They stood and looked at it. The
entrance was dark and quiet. Not a sound was to be heard except for the
wind in the trees. "There it is," said Michael. "The Cave of Mystery."

"Rather thrilling," said Harry. "Jolly good place to keep a prisoner
in. Nobody ever comes here, I should think. I suppose they've tied the
prisoner up. Poor fellow! It must be awful to be kept here day after day
in a dark cave. Do you suppose it's somebody who has been kidnapped
and held to ransom?"

"Gracious!" said Janet. "Do things like that *really* happen nowadays?"

"Of course," said Mark. "Now come on—we'll go in very quietly, just in *case* there's a keeper there—that man you saw yesterday, or somebody else. They might perhaps have someone keeping guard on the prisoner."

Things began to seem even more thrilling. The four children went quietly into the cave, the beams of their torches flashing brightly.

"There's the bed of bracken we made," said Michael, shining his torch on to the tumbled pile of bracken. "We were there, pretending to be shipwrecked sailors sleeping when the man came in."

But Harry and Mark weren't interested in the bracken. They wanted to see what was at the back of the cave. Soon they were shining their torches there, and saw the small, dark opening in the rocky wall.

"Yes—this leads to somewhere," said Harry. "Come on—let's squeeze through. I say—this is exciting, isn't it!"

Harry went through the rather narrow opening first. Janet went next, then Michael, then Mark. They found themselves in a dark passage smelling very damp. Its walls were wet with moisture, and in some places the roof was so low that their heads brushed against it.

The passage wound along for some way. At one place they had to climb over a mound of earth. Harry flashed his torch up to the roof and pointed there. "See," he whispered, "there's been a roof-fall just here.

The walls of the passage were wet with moisture, and in some places the roof was so low that their heads brushed against it.

And then they heard the mournful sound again! The children
stood as if they were frozen.

Let's hope one doesn't come whilst we're in the passage. It would be
awful if we were cut off by a fall of earth."

This was a dreadful thought, and Janet didn't like it at all. She half
thought she would turn back and wait for the boys when they returned.
But no—she couldn't possibly do that. They would say scornfully that
that was just like a girl! So Janet went on with the boys.

And then they heard the mournful sounds again! They came echoing
up the passage, half howl, half moan, and died away into what sounded
like miserable whimpers. The children stood as if they were frozen. The
prisoner must indeed be unhappy if he cried out like that!

"Shall we go on?" whispered Michael. "Or—or shall we turn back?"

Nobody particularly wanted to go on at that moment, but on the other
hand nobody wanted to leave the mystery unsolved! They must go on—it
was the only thing to do.

So on they went, and almost at once came out into a vast cave with a
sandy floor. It seemed much drier than the outside cave and the passage.
The roof rose high, and in places the children's torches could not pick it
up. They stood in awe, looking round. There seemed something very
grand and mysterious about such a large cave. Perhaps it had been used by
animals scores of thousands of years back—and then by men and their
families sheltering here safely from storm and cold and fierce animals.

The children saw that a big stone was rolled in front of the entrance to another cave.

"We should find plenty of bones and things here if we had time to look," whispered Harry. And then he jumped because his whisper was taken up by the echoes in the cave and a great whispering sounded all round them, fading away at last.

"Gracious!" said Janet, startled into speech.

"Shus, shus, shus," said the echoes at once. They were repeating the last part of "Gracious".

And then the noises started again, but this time the howls and groans were taken by the echoes and magnified so tremendously that the whole cave seemed to be full of prisoners moaning, whimpering and howling. The four children clutched one another, holding their breath.

"Goodness—where did that noise come from?" said Mark, the echoes fastening on his words as he spoke them.

"From over there," said Harry. "Come on. I think I can see something." They went over to where his torch shone its straight beam. The children saw that a big stone was rolled in front of the entrance to another cave—a small cave evidently, for the top of the opening was only as high as their waists.

"That's where the prisoner is," said Mark, excited. "Look—here's some water spilt just outside. The man must have spilt that when he brought the jug here yesterday."

"Shall we call to the prisoner?" said Janet.

"Yes," said Harry. "Hey there! Are you a prisoner? Who are you?"

There was no answer at all—yet the four children felt certain that the prisoner was listening intently. In fact, they could all hear his quick breathing as they listened for an answer. And then Janet suddenly felt sure she could hear *two* people breathing. Yes—she could!

"I believe there are *two* prisoners in there," she said. "Why don't they answer us?"

Mark called loudly. "We're friends. You don't need to be afraid. We're just going to roll away this stone and then you'll be free."

Still no answer. How very queer! Surely the prisoners could just call out, "Set us free," or something like that!

But they didn't. Except for their quick breathing, which almost seemed to be a panting, there was no sound from them at all.

The children began to have doubts about moving away the stone. What kind of prisoners were these? They really must be mad not to answer friends who were willing to rescue them. Then Mark made up his mind.

"We'll move the stone a little way," he said, "and shine our torches in. Then we shall see what prisoners are there. We can roll the stone back quickly if we don't like the look of them."

"I wonder why *they* don't move the stone themselves," said Michael suddenly. "It seems jolly queer."

"Their hands are bound, I expect," said Mark. "Now come on, Harry. Help me to shift this stone a bit." Harry helped him, and the stone moved a little from the entrance.

"Come on, Harry. Help me to shift this stone a bit." Harry helped him, and the stone moved a little from the entrance.

At the back of the little cave stood two beautiful dogs, greyhounds.

Then Mark shone his torch in at the crack. He gave a sudden exclamation, and Janet screamed! Four eyes gleamed at them from the darkness at the back of a small cave—fierce eyes, angry eyes! Janet wanted to run away.

"Why—they're animals," said Harry in the greatest surprise. "Not men at all. Here, shine your torch in, Michael; and you, too, Janet. We'll make a better light then to see what the prisoners really are."

At the back of the little cave stood two beautiful dogs, greyhounds, with big, mournful eyes and long noses. They were too frightened to move as the light of the four torches shone into their eyes.

"Look at that—dogs! *Greyhounds!*" said Mark, amazed. "No wonder they didn't shout out to us when we shouted to them. No wonder, too, that we couldn't make out what that mournful moaning, howling noise was—it was the poor things howling in misery and loneliness!"

"Oh, poor poor dogs!" said Janet, almost crying. "Get them out, Mark. Pull away the stone. Let them free."

The three boys tugged at the stone and it came away from the cave entrance. But still the dogs wouldn't come out. It was clear that they were cowed and terrified. Janet, suddenly brave because she was so full of pity, crawled in to them. She saw the jug of water upset on the floor, and a dish empty of food. The dogs cowered away from her.

She stroked and petted them. One licked her face timidly, and then they both made up their minds that this was no enemy but a friend. They fell on the little girl with whimpers of delight and licked her till she was wet all over!

"Stolen greyhounds!" said Harry grimly. "Champions, I expect. Kept here till the hue and cry after them died down, and then they would be shipped across to Ireland or somewhere and sold for large sums."

"Let's take the poor things home with us," begged Janet. "I'm sure they must want a drink—their jug of water is upset."

The two dogs pressed closely against the little girl as the four children went across the vast cave to the little passage. They were soon out in the first cave and then made their way thankfully into the open air. The dogs soon found their high spirits and gambolled about.

How surprised the children's parents were to see them arriving with two beautiful greyhounds, and to hear their strange story. The police were told at once, and two men were sent up to the cave to watch for the man who brought the food and water.

"They'll catch him all right," said the inspector, fondling the lovely dogs. "There's been a lot of this dog-stealing lately. I shall soon be able to find out who are the owners of these beauties!"

They were soon out in the first cave and then made their way thankfully into the open air.

One day a small box arrived, with air-holes in it—and what do you suppose
the children found in the box when they opened it?

"Can we keep them if you don't find out?" asked Janet eagerly. But,
of course, the owners were found that very evening, and the children had
to say goodbye to the two prisoners they had rescued.

That wasn't quite the end of the story, though. One day a small box
arrived, with air-holes in it—and what do you suppose the children found
in the box when they opened it? Yes—a tiny greyhound puppy, the dearest
little thing you ever saw! It was for Janet and Michael, because they had
really been the ones to discover the prisoners.

"But, of course, we'll share him with you, Mark and Harry," said
Janet. "He shall belong to all four of us."

So he does—and I wish he belonged to me, too!

SANTA CLAUS GETS BUSY

"R-r-r-r-RING! R-r-r-r-ring! R-r-r-r-ring!"

"Bother this telephone bell!" said Santa Claus crossly. "As soon as I try to take a nap it wakes me up! First it was the rocking-horse room phoning because they hadn't got enough tails for the horses; then it was the golliwog room because they'd lost two of the biggest . . ."

He lifted up the receiver, put it to his ear and listened.

"WHAT? Gone off with my reindeer? I never heard such a thing. Get them back at once! AT ONCE! How can I go out next week with my sack of toys and my sleigh if I haven't got my reindeer to pull me?"

He crashed the receiver down on the table. "What next? Someone's gone off with my reindeer! How dare they! I really don't know what people are coming to nowadays!" said Santa Claus angrily.

Outside in the stables where the reindeer were kept there was a great to-do. Jingle, the head stable-man, was staring at the empty stalls, going from one to the other, as if he couldn't believe his eyes. Get-Up, his under-man, stamped up and down, talking loudly, whilst the stable-lads listened in awe.

"How did I know he meant to go off with the reindeer? He just came and said he could put a special polish on their hooves that would make them go twice as fast. And as Santa Claus always complains the reindeer are too slow I thought I'd try the polish."

"Yes—and you let him try the reindeer, too, you silly, stupid fellow!" suddenly roared the head stable-man. "Told him to take the

153

"You hold your tongues," roared Jingle. "I go to get my dinner and when I come back they've gone!"

reindeer up into the sky, and you'd time them and see if they really did go any faster than usual."

"And up he went," said a stable-lad.

"With all the reindeer," said another.

"And he never came back!" said the third.

"You hold your tongues," roared Jingle. "I go off to get my dinner and leave Get-Up and three lads here to see to the reindeer—and when I come back they've gone! Right under your noses! What did you want to trust a fellow like that for, with his tale of a wonderful hoof-polish! Wait till I get my whip. I'll polish you all with that."

Certainly it was a strange and tiresome thing to happen just in Christmas week. The merry-eyed tramp who had come to the stable door had tricked everyone easily.

He had solemnly rubbed the reindeer's hooves with some kind of yellow polish which he said would make them gallop through the sky twice as fast—and then he had leapt on to the biggest one and taken the whole lot up into the sky, whilst Get-Up stood below, looking at his watch to time their speed.

And, to everyone's open-mouthed amazement, the reindeer had galloped into a deep purple cloud, their hooves thundering as they went—and had disappeared for good! The wicked fellow had stolen them away.

"We'll have to get them back," groaned Jingle. "But how? Where have they gone?"

"Better put out a notice all over Toyland asking if anyone has heard the sound of reindeer hooves," said Get-Up. "When the reports come in we can look at a map and find the different places. The one that is farthest away will be the place to look for the reindeer."

But it wasn't any good putting out a notice, because there had been thunderstorms all over the country that day and nobody knew whether it was thunder or reindeer hooves they had heard.

Then messengers were sent out everywhere to see if reindeer had suddenly arrived at somebody's stables. But that wasn't any good, either. Nobody had heard of any strange reindeer arriving anywhere.

Santa Claus grew more and more anxious as Christmas Eve drew near. What was he to do without his reindeer to draw his sleigh?

"We'll send to the zoo and see if they can lend us some," said Jingle in despair. "I'll go myself and find out."

So he went to the zoo and found the keepers of the Reindeer House. They thought Jingle was quite mad.

"My dear fellow, we don't believe in Santa Claus, and if we did we wouldn't allow our reindeer to try and scamper up in the sky," said the

Messengers were sent out everywhere to see if reindeer had suddenly arrived at somebody's stables. But that wasn't any good.

head keeper. "Anyway, they all have very bad coughs and have to be kept indoors."

Jingle went off sadly. It wouldn't do to take reindeer with coughs and colds. They wouldn't be able to go fast at all.

He wondered if the big flamingo birds at the zoo could pull the sleigh. This time he didn't ask the keepers. He went to the enclosure himself when it was dark and got in with the long-legged flamingos.

"Oh yes—set us free!" begged the flamingos. "We can fly strongly."

"Could you pull a sleigh along?" asked Jingle.

"We don't know what it is, but of course we could pull it," said the birds.

"We'll pull it all the way back to our own country," said a small one.

Jingle frowned. "Oh no—you wouldn't have to take the sleigh to your own country," he said. "You'd have to take it to the roofs of houses."

"What a silly idea!" chorused the birds. "We should fly straight off to our own country."

Jingle sighed and said no more. He left the flamingos and went out of the zoo. It would never do to use birds that wouldn't take Santa Claus where he wanted to go. How angry he would be to land in some strange, far-off land he didn't know at all, with not a house in sight!

"My dear fellow, we don't believe in Santa Claus, and if we did we wouldn't allow our reindeer to try and scamper up in the sky," said the head keeper.

"Sir!" he said suddenly to Santa Claus. "Why don't you hire an
aeroplane? That would easily take all the toys."

Jingle went to see Santa Claus. "It's no good, sir," he said. "I
haven't been able to solve our problem at all. Can't get our own reindeer
back because we don't know where they are; can't get the zoo reindeer—
and nothing else seems possible."

A small brownie was in the room. He had come from the toy-aeroplane room to tell Santa Claus that some of the aeroplanes wanted a good
talking to because they wouldn't fly properly. He listened to all that
Jingle was saying.

"Sir!" he said suddenly to Santa Claus. "Why don't you hire an aeroplane? That would easily take all the toys. You could hire a pilot, too,
to take you."

"Now why didn't we think of that before?" said Santa Claus. "Jingle,
please see to it. And choose a pilot who has children of his own, because
he won't mind stopping on every roof."

But the pilots Jingle went to said the same thing to him each time.
"We can't land on a roof! You must be mad! Don't you know that

aeroplanes must have good landing grounds with long runways? Anyway, we'd probably break the roofs if we did try to land!"

And then Jingle at last heard of something he thought would do. It was the little brownie from the toy-aeroplane room that told him.

"Please, Mr. Jingle, sir, I've got an idea," he said. "You know we make model toy aeroplanes, don't you? We've got every kind there is. And we've got a toy model of a thing called a helicopter. It has propellers above it, sir, instead of at the front—and it can land like a bird, hovering first, and then going gently down to land on a small space. Sir, what about a helicopter?"

Jingle went to see the toy helicopter. It certainly looked very good. The brownie set it going and it went up into the air, its propellers whirring above it. Then it came slowly down towards a big doll's-house the brownie had set nearby. It hovered a second or two over the roof and then quietly settled on it.

"There you are, Mr. Jingle, sir!" said the brownie, very pleased. "Get a helicopter for Santa Claus, and he can easily land on every roof and get down the chimney with his toys. It won't annoy him by stamping hooves on tiles either, like his reindeer did last year."

"It's certainly an idea," said Jingle. "I'll make inquiries about a helicopter."

But will you believe it, nobody would let him hire a helicopter for Santa Claus. They said helicopters weren't meant to land on roofs on Christmas Eve, and would Jingle please take his silly ideas somewhere else? He was very upset indeed.

It came slowly down towards a big doll's-house the brownie had set nearby.

He said the right words, touched the toy helicopter with his hands, and then threw
a magic powder over the little machine.

He went to tell Santa Claus that he had come to the end of his ideas.
It wasn't any good trying anything else. Santa Claus would just have to
miss out Christmas for once.

Santa Claus stared at Jingle in amazement. "What are you talking
about, my good fellow? Miss out *Christmas*? Disappoint the children?
Waste all the toys we've been working on? You must be mad!"

Jingle was offended. "Well, sir, I've done everything I can think of.
Perhaps *you* can think of something."

"Yes, I can," said Santa Claus at once. "I'll get one of the toy helicopters, use magic to make it big enough for me, and go off in that. I
don't see why it shouldn't be as good as a real one."

Well, that certainly was an idea! Santa Claus didn't have to use a
great deal of magic, really. He said the right words, touched the toy
helicopter with his hands, and then threw a magic powder over the little
machine. It swelled up at once. The brownies in the aeroplane room
watched in astonishment. Why, it was as big as a real helicopter!

Actually, it wasn't nearly as big. Santa Claus made it just the right
size to take him and his sack. He got into the machine and settled himself down comfortably.

Yes, it was just the right size. He could manage it nicely. The brownie
told him in excitement just how to work it.

"I'll take a trial flight now," said Santa Claus boldly, and he pulled down a lever. The helicopter made a purring noise and its propellers swung round over his head. It rose from the floor. He flew round and round the enormous aeroplane room and then came to ground again. He stepped out.

"Very nice. Exactly what I want. It will be no trouble at all to fly, and it will land beautifully on the very smallest roof. I'll have to make it small again, carry it out into the open, and make it big there. I couldn't possibly get it through the door or window here."

"Yes, sir," said the brownie.

"Jingle," said Santa Claus, turning to him, "see that my sack is put ready in my helicopter on Christmas Eve, and look over the machine to make sure it's all right. If my reindeer are not found before then I'll use the helicopter on Christmas Eve."

"Whatever will the children say if you don't arrive pulled by your reindeer?" said Jingle.

"They won't know," said Santa Claus. "They will all be asleep. I shall arrive in my helicopter, land on the roof, and go down the chimney just as usual—and not a single child will know there's a helicopter on the roof! Aha!"

And he went off, leaving Jingle in charge.

Christmas Eve is already here. The reindeer haven't come back—so the helicopter will purr through the sky with Santa Claus and his sack of toys. You oughn't to peep—but I thought you might like to *listen*!

R-r-r-r-r! R-r-r-r-r-r-r! Bumpity-bump. Yes, that's the helicopter on your roof. What an extraordinary thing!

Penguins are comical birds, and most amusing to watch. Their wings cannot be used for flying, but are like flippers. They swim very well in the water, and their flippers are useful then.

I'LL DO THEM TOMORROW

LINNIE was a plump little pixie girl who lived in a tiny cottage in the middle of Pat-a-cake Village. It was a pretty little cottage, with red and pink roses climbing outside, and big hollyhocks waving by the walls.

But inside the cottage was very different! Goodness me, how dirty it was! The floor wanted scrubbing. The curtains wanted washing. The windows wanted cleaning, and everything looked as if it needed a good brushing and dusting.

"You *are* a lazy little thing, Linnie," said her neighbour, Dame Trot-About. "Why don't you clean your kettle and your saucepans?"

"Linnie, why don't you do a little hard work?" cried her other neighbour, Mother Lucy. "Look at your curtains! They are a disgrace to the village!"

"I'll do them tomorrow," promised Linnie. But she didn't. She never did any work if she could help it, the lazy little thing.

Then one day her Aunt Jemima sent her five shillings to spend, and Linnie made up her mind to ask old Mrs. Redhands to come along and clean her house for her.

"She will do it for five shillings," thought Linnie. "And then my neighbours will perhaps stop worrying me about my dirty cottage. I'll call in and ask her today."

Mrs. Redhands said yes, certainly she would come along and clean Linnie's cottage for five shillings. So she arrived the next day in a big

tub of water as you do! This little fellow is going to give Mummy a really big squirt as soon as he has filled his trunk.

clean apron and knocked at the door. Linnie opened it. "Come along in!" she said. "I'm afraid the cottage *is* rather dirty—but, you see, I haven't had time to clean it for some weeks."

Mrs. Redhands looked round the rooms. "Good gracious!" she said in great disgust. "I never saw such a mess in my life. I can't do all this in a day. You will have to let me come tomorrow as well."

"But I can't pay you for two days," said Linnie.

"Well, you must help me, then," said Mrs. Redhands. "First of all, where's the soap and the scrubbing-brush?"

"I forgot to get the soap,"

"Good gracious!" she said in great disgust.
"I never saw such a mess in my life."

said Linnie, "but here's the scrubbing-brush." She held out a very old one and Mrs. Redhands shook her head at once.

"No use at all," she said. "You must go out and get a new one—and some soap, too. Now hurry, for goodness' sake, because I want to start!"

She rushed Linnie out of the front door, and the pixie ran quite fast. She bought the soap, a scrubbing-brush, a new broom, and a duster, for she was afraid that Mrs. Redhands would think she needed those too.

"Now go and fill the pail with hot water for me!" cried Mrs. Redhands, rolling her sleeves up. "Hurry, Linnie! Bring it to me here—and put some more coke on the fire, please, to keep the water hot."

Linnie filled the pail and carried it to Mrs. Redhands, puffing and panting. Then she put some coke on the fire. After that she picked up the paper and sat down to read it.

"Linnie, Linnie!" called Mrs. Redhands. "Come and clear this room for me. I can't scrub the floor with all these rugs about. Roll them up for me and take them into the garden. And you might hang them on the line and give them a bang to get the dust out."

Linnie went to roll up the rugs. They were so dusty that they made her cough. She hung them on the line and then fetched the carpet-beater. But she didn't like the hard work and soon gave up.

"Can't you beat the carpets properly?" called Mrs. Redhands. "Well, I'll do that for you—but you must clean away the cobwebs from the ceiling if I do that. Here's the broom."

Linnie found herself sweeping away heaps of cobwebs. They fell on her pretty golden hair. She was horrified to see how many cobwebs there were. She wrapped a hanky round her head, and swept away some more cobwebs.

"Oh dear! Why ever did I let my cottage get so dirty?" she thought. "Oooh—there's a great big spider. Go away, Eight-Legs, go away!"

The spider ran straight at Linnie, and she called to Mrs. Redhands. "Oh, come and finish doing the cobwebs—I don't like spiders."

"Can't you beat the carpets properly?" called Mrs. Redhands.
"Well, I'll do that for you."

"Well, I've finished the rugs, so I'll come and do the ceilings," said Mrs. Redhands, bustling in. "Now, my dear, what's for dinner? I do a good morning's work and it makes me hungry. I'm not having anything out of a tin, let me tell you—I want a well-cooked dinner."

"Well, what would you like to cook?" asked Linnie.

"My dear, *you're* going to do the cooking!" said Mrs. Redhands. "Don't make any mistake about that! I've come here to clean your dirty cottage, not to cook a dinner for myself."

So Linnie had to peel potatoes, fetch some chops from the butcher, and get ready a steamed treacle pudding. Goodness, she hadn't worked so hard for months!

She did enjoy her dinner—just as much as Mrs. Redhands did. Afterwards she had to wash up, and then Mrs. Redhands called to her.

"Linnie! These curtains must be washed. They are so black that I don't know what colour they are supposed to be! Take them all down and put them in to soak for me whilst I finish cleaning out this room."

"Oh dear!" thought Linnie, running to get the wash-tub. "How hard I am working today! Why ever did I get Mrs. Redhands in? I'm doing more work today than I did for weeks."

She took down all the curtains. She put them to soak. Then she found that she had let the kitchen fire out; and as Mrs. Redhands said she really

So Linnie had to peel potatoes, fetch some chops from the butcher,
and get ready a steamed treacle pudding.

must have more hot water, Linnie had to light it again. Then she had to give Mrs. Redhands a hand in hanging out the curtains.

"They will be dry enough to iron after tea," said Mrs. Redhands happily. "You and I can do that together, Linnie."

"Oh dear! Can't they be left till tomorrow?" said Linnie. "I'm so tired."

"Tired! Nonsense! You've had quite a lazy day compared with me," said Mrs. Redhands. "And I shouldn't *think* of leaving the curtains. Very lazy thing to do. That's what's been the matter with you, Linnie, I can see— you leave things till tomorrow —and then they never get done.

Linnie had to give Mrs. Redhands a hand in hanging out the curtains.

No wonder your cottage is the dirtiest in the whole of the village."

Linnie went red. She didn't like hearing that. She put the irons on the stove to warm and hoped that the curtains wouldn't take long to do.

But good Mrs. Redhands hadn't only washed the curtains! She had washed the covers and the bedspreads, too. Those had to be ironed, and, dear me, what a long time they took!

"Now you hang up the curtains, Linnie, whilst I put everything away," said Mrs. Redhands.

So poor Linnie had to get out the step-ladder and hang up all the clean curtains on their hooks. Dear me, she could hardly walk across the room when she had finished.

"Good!" said Mrs. Redhands. "Now I really think everything is done. May I have my five shillings, please, Linnie?"

"Yes, here it is," said Linnie, giving the money to Mrs. Redhands. "Thank you for your hard work."

"If you like I will come every week and give you a hand," said kind Mrs. Redhands. "I can't bear to think of this little cottage getting all dirty again. We could easily do it together in one day—then if you want to be lazy for the rest of the week, you can."

"I'm *not* lazy!" cried Linnie crossly. "I'm not. And I'd rather you didn't come each week, Mrs. Redhands, thank you. I can keep my cottage clean myself."

"Well, well—I'll just look in each Saturday morning and see how it's keeping," said Mrs. Redhands, pinning on her hat. "Good night, Linnie."

Linnie sank down into her chair, quite tired out. "Oh dear, oh dear!" she sighed. "It's far harder work to have Mrs. Redhands in than it would be to do the work myself each day! Good gracious me—my legs are so tired that I can hardly get myself to bed!"

She did get to bed, and she fell fast asleep at once. And all night long she dreamt that she was working very hard indeed for Mrs. Redhands.

When she woke up she looked round her clean, pretty bedroom and made a promise to herself.

"I won't have Mrs. Redhands coming round every Saturday and making me work hard for her. I'll just work hard for myself each day. It won't be nearly so tiring!"

So that's what Linnie does now—and when Mrs. Redhands pops her head in at the door on Saturday morning she is always surprised to see such a spick-and-span cottage.

"Goodness gracious!" she says. "You *have* turned over a new leaf!"

And Linnie certainly has!

Linnie sank down into her chair, quite tired out.
"Oh dear, oh dear!" she sighed.

THE PACKET OF SWEETS

"I SAY!" said Bill, coming into the cloakroom where the others were hanging up their hats and changing their shoes. "I say! Look what I've found!"

The others crowded round. Bill held out a little blue packet. He opened the top of it, and inside the children saw a lot of little round yellow things.

"Sweets!" said Bill. "Somebody bought them and dropped them. I found them out in the road, so I expect they fell from someone's bicycle basket. Have one?"

"But you ought to try to find out who they belong to before you eat them," said Mollie at once.

"Finding's keeping," said Bill.

"It isn't," said George. "You know it isn't. Suppose you found a diamond brooch. Would you say it was yours just because you found it? You'd have to take it to the police station, you know you would."

"Well, I guess the police would laugh if I took these sweets along," said Bill.

"I don't care. You ought to," said George. "Or at least you should hand them over to our teacher. She would know what was best to do—and if she couldn't find out who the owner was she'd give them back to you. But you certainly ought to make enquiries before you eat them."

"Finding's keeping," said Bill again obstinately. "My mother says so."

"Then she's not much good as a mother if that's the kind of thing she teaches you," said George, beginning to lose his temper. "No wonder you tell fibs and cheat if that's the kind of mother you've got. No wonder you——"

"If you say another word I'll hit you!" shouted Bill— but just then the teacher came in and looked in surprise at the angry boys and the listening children.

"Didn't you hear the bell?" she said. "Come along in at once—and take those scowls off your faces, Bill and George."

Bill put on an even bigger scowl when the teacher went out. He stuffed the little packet

"If you say another word I'll hit you!" shouted Bill.

he had found into the satchel he had hung on his peg.

"I'll give you all a sweet at playtime," he said. "All except goody-goody George."

George turned away. He was sorry he had lost his temper now—and, after all, if Bill had the kind of mother who taught him wrong things he supposed Bill couldn't really help believing them. George felt glad his mother was different. You could always trust what she said.

At playtime Bill went to his satchel and got out the little packet. He ran into the playground with it.

"Come on—share them with me!" he cried. "There'll be two or three for everyone!"

George called to his little sister. "Sue! Don't you take one!"

"Of course I'm not going to," said Sue.

"Nor am I," said Ronnie. "I think the same as you, George."

"So do I," said Mark, and Fred and Connie said the same.

But Harry, Tom, Lennie, Joan and Betty came round Bill to share the sweets. Harry was greedy and took three. Bill was greedy, too, and he took three. The others had one each.

"They're not very nice, are they, when the first sweetness has been sucked off?" said Joan, and she spat hers out. "Funny sort of sweets. I don't like them."

Bill didn't like Joan spitting hers out, because it made George laugh. So he went on sucking his, but he swallowed them before he had quite finished them because they really did taste nasty.

Harry swallowed his, too, because he liked to do everything that Bill did. Tom, Lennie and Betty sucked theirs almost to the end, and then swallowed them quickly.

"I don't believe they are such nice sweets after all," said George with a laugh.

"Well, they are then," said Bill at once, and he took another sweet and popped it into his mouth. He handed the packet to Harry. Harry shook his head.

None of the others would take a sweet, either. Bill stuffed the packet into his pocket, and when he thought no one was looking he spat out the last sweet he had in his mouth. It certainly wasn't nice after the first few sucks.

Bill didn't like Joan spitting hers out, because it made George laugh.
So he went on sucking his.

"I feel awful," said Bill, leaning his head on his hand. "Oh, Miss Brown, I do feel
so ill. I want to be sick."

Everyone went in when the bell rang. It was a nice lesson that morning after playtime, one that everyone liked, because it was story-time.
The teacher was reading the tales of Robin Hood, and they were very
exciting.

The children settled down to listen. Miss Brown began reading.

Suddenly some of the children began to fidget. Miss Brown looked up
with a frown. She glanced round the class of twelve children, and then
she put down the book.

"Bill! Harry! Tom! What's the matter? Don't you feel well? You
look so pale."

"I feel awful," said Bill, leaning his head on his hand. "Oh, Miss
Brown, I do feel so ill. I want to be sick."

"George, take Bill outside," said Miss Brown. "Harry, do you feel
sick, too?"

"I feel—funny," said Harry. "My head's funny. My throat's funny.
Miss Brown, I want to be sick, too."

Then Tom gave a groan, and Lennie began to cry because he felt ill and
frightened. Betty looked very white, and Joan held her head in her hands.

"What *is* the matter with you children?" said Miss Brown, in alarm.
"Oh, Harry! Help him, somebody—he's fallen off his chair! Fred, help
me to lay him flat on the floor. Put a cushion under his head. Oh dear,
what *can* be the matter?"

"Shall I run across the road and get the doctor?" asked Ronnie. "I know he's in because I just saw his car."

"Yes, you'd better," said Miss Brown, really alarmed now, because certainly some of the children looked very ill indeed.

George came back into the classroom looking frightened. "Miss Brown! You must come to Bill. He's fainted or something."

Miss Brown fled out to poor Bill. Ronnie ran for the doctor. He was just going out again but he came straight across to the school when he heard the news that Ronnie panted out.

He carried Bill back into the classroom and laid him beside Harry. He looked quickly round the room, and saw how ill Lennie, Tom and Betty looked. Joan was white, too.

"What's happened?" he asked Miss Brown. "These children have been poisoned, Miss Brown. What have they been eating?"

"*Poisoned!*" said Miss Brown, amazed. "Oh dear! Children, what have you been eating?"

Neither Bill nor Harry could answer; they were far too ill. George answered instead.

"*I* know what it is—it's those sweets Bill found this morning! He had three or four, so did Harry. The others only had one—and Joan spat hers out. The rest of us wouldn't have them."

"What sweets? Quick, show me," said the doctor. George felt in Bill's pocket and brought out the little blue packet.

Ronnie ran for the doctor. He was just going out again.

171

The doctor opened it and looked at the little yellow things inside. "Good gracious—what are we to do! These are pills—poisonous to young children! The chemist's boy must have dropped them on his delivery round this morning. Miss Brown, I must get these children into my car and take them straight to hospital. I'm afraid these two boys on the floor are very dangerously ill."

Sue and Connie began to cry. George helped the doctor to carry Bill and Harry to the car. They couldn't even walk. Tom, Lennie, Joan and Betty were helped along. They were all very, very frightened.

The doctor went off with them in his car. Miss Brown and the other children went back to the classroom. "We can't do any more lessons this morning," she said in a shaky voice. "I must telephone to the mothers of those poor children. Oh, I hope they'll be all right. How *silly* to eat things like that! If only Bill had brought the packet to me, as he should have done, I could have told him at once they were pills and probably poisonous."

The doctor went off with them in his car. Miss Brown and the other children went back to the classroom.

George's mother put her arms round George and Sue. "Oh, George—Sue! I *am* glad you didn't take one of those sweets."

The children went home, solemn and scared. They poured out the story to their mothers, who looked very solemn, too. George's mother put her arms round George and Sue.

"Oh, George—Sue! I *am* glad you didn't take one of those sweets. Thank goodness you didn't."

"Well, you should thank yourself for that," said George. "You've always said that if we find anything we shouldn't keep it but try our best to find who lost it. And I was cross with Bill because he said 'Oh, finding's keeping'—and, of course, I wouldn't take one of the sweets, and neither would Sue. We remembered what you said"

"And Bill remembered what *his* mother said, and took the sweets for his own," said Sue. "His mother can't be very honest, Mummy—and so I suppose Bill isn't either."

"You mustn't say things like that," said her mother, though secretly she thought that Sue was perfectly right. "Poor Bill! I'm afraid he will be terribly ill."

He was. And so was Harry, because the two of them had eaten so many of the pills. Lennie and Tom and Betty had to stay in hospital for a day and night, and then they were better and went home. Joan wasn't very ill because she had been sensible enough to spit out her "sweet", and she went home that afternoon. But poor Bill and Harry are still in hospital, and are feeling very ill and miserable. George and Sue go to see them and

"I feel as if I shall never be right again!" says poor Bill. "If only I'd believed you when you said 'Finding's *not* keeping!'"

take them books and flowers, and when the two boys see them coming in, their cheeks red and their eyes bright, they look at them with envy.

"I feel as if I shall never be right again!" says poor Bill. "Oh, George —if only I'd believed you when you said 'Finding's *not* keeping!' I wouldn't have been the cause of making the others ill, too, then. I'll never do such a thing again, never! It was wrong as well as foolish."

"I wish somebody would write all this down so that other children would know what happened to us, and be warned," said Harry from his bed. "I'd like children everywhere to know. I would really."

Well, Harry was right, of course, and it was a good idea of his to want somebody to write their story. I thought I'd better do it—just in *case* there are still a few children who think that Finding is Keeping, and that they can eat anything they find.

Wasn't it a dreadful thing to happen?

Answer to puzzle on page 43

S	T	A	R
N	A	M	E
O	P	E	N
W	E	N	T

Answer to puzzle on page 54
FROGSPAWN

Answers to puzzles on page 136
(1) STRAY—TRAY—RAY—AY.
(2) PAIL—NAIL—TAIL.

JOSIE, CLICK and BUN Give a Party

YOU REMEMBER Josie, Click and Bun, don't you, who live in the **little** Train House together? Josie is the curly-haired doll, Bun is the **toy** bunny, and Click is the clockwork mouse. Well, this is the story **of** what happened one winter afternoon.

They were going to give a party. It had been very cold, dull **weather,** there had been nothing to do, and Bun and Click were getting **rather** naughty. So Josie thought it would be a good idea to give a party.

"We'll have a very nice time," she said to Bun and Click. "I'll **make** some lovely cakes, and you two can make some pretty decorations **for the** rooms. I'll get out the balloons and you can blow them up. Now **stop** being naughty and we'll all be happy together."

Well, they sent out cards to Jinky, the elf, and Frisky, the **squirrel,** and Pippy, the pixie, and to Bun's cousin, Miss Flop-Ears. They **all** lived in the next village and they said they would come on the **four-** o'clock bus.

"I've made some lovely sandwiches," said Josie when the great **day** came. "And I've made a cake with candles on it. There are chocolate-iced buns with your names on. And look at the sweets I've made!"

"You're very, very clever, Josie," said Bun. "We shall have a **lovely** time. Will you tie my bow for me, ready for the party? I can't make **it** look nice."

Well, Josie tied his new red bow, and she tied Click's yellow one, **and** then she put on her party frock. It was very frilly and looked **nice.**

Everything looked nice—the table set with dishes of lovely things to eat, the crackers beside each plate, the balloons hanging round the little room, and the decorations that Bun and Click had made.

"I do feel so happy!" squealed Click, tearing about the room. "Josie, wind me up, will you? I've run about such a lot that I'm almost run down."

Well, you would think that everything was happy and merry and just right, wouldn't you—but it wasn't. *Nobody came at four o'clock!* There was Josie at the door, ready to welcome everybody—and nobody arrived!

"What's happened?" she wondered, looking out of the door. "Certainly there is snow on the ground—but that wouldn't stop the others from catching the bus—and we've swept a path right to our front gate."

"They don't like us. They don't want to come," said Bun, suddenly getting gloomy.

"I shall go and see if they are coming down the road," said Click, and before the others could stop him he shot down the path and out into the snowy road.

There was Josie at the door, ready to welcome everybody—and nobody arrived!

"Click! Come back! You know you always get stuck in the snow," called Josie crossly. But Click was halfway down the road to the bus-stop.

And of course he *did* get stuck in the snow! He ran straight into a very deep bit, and there he stopped. "Help! I'm stuck! Help me, Josie!" he squealed.

Josie slipped on her coat and ran out. Bun followed her. It took quite a time to find Click, because he had gone even deeper into the snow, and his squeals could no longer be heard.

Bun found him quite by accident. He trod on him! "Here he is!" he cried, and

"Who's been here? Somebody's been in and stolen our goodies whilst we were out in the road. We've got nothing for our guests to eat."

began to dig him out. Click was crying because Bun had trodden so hard on him.

"Well, it serves you right," said Josie. "You know I don't like you to run out in the snow, Click. Now stop crying and come back. Perhaps our guests will come on the next bus."

"Oh yes," said Bun, cheering up. "Of course they will. A-TISH-oo!"

"There! Bun's caught cold coming out in the snow to help you," said Josie, vexed. "Bun, do you feel as if you've got a cold already?"

"Yes. A-tish-OO!" said Bun. "I'm afraid I have. But please don't make me go to bed before the party, Josie."

They went back indoors, Click still crying, Bun sneezing and Josie scolding. And what a shock they got when they went indoors!

The sandwiches were gone. The cakes were gone. The balloons had disappeared and so had the crackers. And the lovely big cake with candles was gone too. Josie looked at the table in horror.

"Who's been here? Somebody's been in and stolen our goodies whilst we were out in the road. We've got nothing for our guests to eat when they come!"

"It's all my fault," wailed Click. "If I hadn't run out this wouldn't have happened."

"A-tish-oooooooo," said Bun, dismally.

Josie nearly cried. "Oh dear, oh dear—here's all our tea stolen, Bun with a cold, and four guests coming on the next bus."

"*Who* could have stolen everything?" said Bun, looking round. "Oooh, I say—what's that?"

She suddenly swept the squalling cat into the cupboard.

He pointed with his paw at a black heap in front of the fire. Josie stared. Click gave a scream and backed into a corner.

"It's a cat!" he squealed. "A big black cat. Chase him away before he eats me."

"He must be the thief," said Bun, not stopping to think that a cat wouldn't eat crackers and balloons. "He's had all the cakes and sandwiches. Wicked cat! Shoo!"

The cat untucked its head and looked at the angry rabbit out of bright-green eyes. "I lost my way in the snow," he said. "I came in for shelter and warmth."

"You're a bad, wicked cat," said Josie, and she took up her broom. "Go away! Shoo!"

She swept the cat into a corner. It put out its claws and spat. It simply wouldn't be swept out of the house. It went and sat down by the fire again, its green eyes gleaming brightly.

Bun opened a cupboard door. He nodded at Josie, and she suddenly swept the squalling cat into the cupboard. Bun slammed the door and locked it. Aha! The cat was caught.

"Now, if we can find out who the cat belongs to we can tell all about his greediness and make his mistress pay for the damage," said Josie. "I never heard of such a thing! A cat walking in like that and eating absolutely everything."

"Except the cream and the milk," said Click, peeping into the jugs. "What a queer cat! Did he eat the balloons, too, do you think?"

178

The cat began to make a tremendous noise in the cupboard. He squalled and miaowed and spat and clawed at the door.

"He's gone mad," said Bun. "A-tish-oo!"

"Oh dear. Get a clean hanky, Bun," said Josie. "You *really* ought to go to bed. Whatever are we to do with all those guests coming and no party?"

Then they all jumped dreadfully, because a voice spoke out of the air.

"What have you done with my cat?"

Josie, Click and Bun stared all round the room. Who was speaking? There was nobody there but themselves! Click ran under the table in a fright. Bun took hold of Josie's hand. He was trembling.

"Who's speaking?" he said to Josie. "I can't see anyone."

"WHAT HAVE YOU DONE WITH MY CAT?" said the voice again—and then someone began to appear in the room, bit by bit—first his feet, then his legs, then his middle, then his hands and arms, and last of all his head!

And WHO do you suppose it was? Can you guess? It was old Pink-Whistle, that kind little man, half-human, half-brownie, who goes about the world to see what wrong things he can put right!

But how angry he looked now! He pointed to the cupboard. "You've shut my cat in there. You are unkind and cruel. He came out for a walk with me and got lost in the snow. You might have let him wait here in the warm till I came."

Josie stared at Mr. Pink-Whistle as if she couldn't believe her eyes. Then she ran to him. "I know who you are! I've often read stories about

He pointed to the cupboard. "You've shut my cat in there. You are unkind and cruel. He came out for a walk with me and got lost."

"I met the red goblins down the road, and they were carrying cakes and balloons and sandwiches. I thought it was very peculiar."

you. You're Mr. Pink-Whistle, dear kind Pink-Whistle! Oh, I didn't know it was *your* cat!"

Bun went to the door of the cupboard and opened it. Out sprang the black cat at once. Mr. Pink-Whistle bent down to stroke him. "Poor old Sooty! Why did they treat you like that then?"

Josie explained, going rather red. "We went out for just a few minutes and left the door open. And when we came back all our nice goodies were gone—and as Sooty was here we thought he'd had them. I'm so sorry!"

"I know who took them," said Pink-Whistle at once. "I met the red goblins down the road, and they were carrying cakes and balloons and sandwiches. I thought it was very peculiar. Well—they must have eaten them all by now, I'm afraid."

"And we've got guests coming to our party by the next bus!" said Josie in despair.

"I can do something about that," said Mr. Pink-Whistle, feeling very cheerful because he had happened on something he could put right. "Just go and look in that cupboard you put Sooty in."

And, will you believe it, the shelves were full of cakes and jellies and trifles and biscuits! And there was a little pile of balloons all waiting to be blown up.

Well, well, well! Click squealed in delight. Josie kissed Pink-Whistle, and Bun actually patted the cat. Then he sneezed loudly.

"Bun! Go to bed at once!" said Josie. "You will be very ill if you don't!"

"Poor Bun!" said Pink-Whistle kindly. "Here, sniff this—it will soon put you right."

He held out a tiny little bottle filled with red liquid. Bun put his nose to it and sniffed. Then he sneezed seventeen times without stopping. When at last he stopped he looked at Josie. "Sneezed my cold all away!" he said. "Not a bit of it left. Thank you very much, Mr. Pink-Whistle."

"Well, you *have* brought us good luck," said Josie, pleased. "Oh, look —there's the robin at the window-sill with a note in his beak."

The note made them all very sad again. "Listen to this," said Josie. "'*Dear Josie, Click and Bun, The snow is so thick in our village that the buses aren't running. So we can't come to your party. We are very, very sorry. Love from Jinky, Pippy, Frisky and Flop-Ears.*'"

"Oh *dear*!" said Josie, almost in tears. "Here we've got a whole lot of lovely things to eat again, and Bun's cold made better—and now our guests aren't coming. What a dreadful disappointment."

"Well," said Mr. Pink-Whistle, "I could send Sooty to fetch three other guests if you like. And if you'd have me and Sooty for guests, too, we could make a very nice party."

"Oh *yes*," said Josie, pleased. "Do send Sooty for some more guests. They are sure to be nice if they are friends of yours."

So off went Sooty through the snow—and do you know who he brought back with him?

So off went Sooty through the snow to fetch three other guests.

He brought Silky, Moonface and the old Saucepan Man! Josie cried out in delight.

"Oh, I've always wanted to meet you! Oh, what a really lovely party!"

"Hearty?" said old Saucepan, mishearing as usual. "Yes, I'm hale and hearty, thank you. Awfully nice of you to ask us out to tea. I've dressed myself up in my very best kettles and saucepans for you!"

Well, they all had a wonderful time. The tea was soon eaten, and because there were not quite enough jellies Josie was sent to the cupboard again—and there on the shelf were two more. How marvellous!

Mr. Pink-Whistle enjoyed himself more than anyone, especially when he was the blind man in blind-man's-buff and caught the old Saucepan Man. He couldn't think *what* he was, and when Josie asked him the name of the person he had caught he said, "I must have caught the kitchen stove," and Click laughed so much that he jerked his key out.

Everyone was given a balloon. Even Sooty had one—he said it was the first balloon he had ever had. Click wasn't a bit afraid of him when he said goodbye, and shook paws as if he were Sooty's very best friend!

"Thank you for your party, Josie," said Mr. Pink-Whistle.

"Oh, Mr. Pink-Whistle, it wasn't *my* party—it was yours!" cried Josie. "Thank *you*, Mr. Pink-Whistle. You are every bit as nice as you are in your stories."

So he is. You'll find that out when you meet him!

Mr. Pink-Whistle enjoyed himself more than anyone, especially when he was the blind man in blind-man's-buff and caught the old Saucepan Man.

INTERFERING INA

I WONDER if you ever knew Interfering Ina? She was a little girl about eight years old, quite pretty, quite clever—but, oh dear, how she did interfere with all the other children!

If she saw two or three of them playing a game together she would go and poke her nose into the game and say, "Oh, you are not playing that quite right! Look, you should play it *this* way!"

And then she would make the children play quite a different way, a way they didn't want to play at all!

"Don't interfere!" they would say at last. "Go away, Ina!"

"Well, I only wanted to put you right," Ina would say, and then off she would go in a huff.

If she saw a little girl sewing she would go at once to see what she was doing. Then she would say, "Oh, you are making an overall for your doll, I see. Well, you are doing it wrong. You should sew like *this*!"

And she would take the sewing from the little girl's hand and make her sew it quite differently. It *was* so tiresome of Ina!

The other children got very tired of her. "Here comes Interfering Ina!" they would say as soon as they saw her coming. "Hallo, Ina. Are you going to poke your nose into our games again? Well, go away."

But do you suppose that cured Ina of her tiresome ways? Not a bit! She simply loved to interfere with everything, and she was so curious about everybody and what they were doing that she was for ever poking her nose here, there and everywhere!

She saw four little brownie-men playing leapfrog! They were having a fine game,
and were shouting and laughing.

Now one day she was walking home alone from school. The other children wouldn't walk with her because she had interfered in a fine new game they had made up that morning and had spoilt it for them. So there was Ina, walking home by herself, feeling very cross indeed.

She came to a field and heard somebody laughing. It was such a funny, high little laugh that Ina stopped to see who it could be. She climbed on the gate and peeped into the field. And there she saw a most surprising sight.

She saw four little brownie-men playing leapfrog! They were having a fine game, and were shouting and laughing in little bird-like voices. Ina watched them for a while and then she called to them.

"You know, that's not the right way to play leapfrog! You want to bend down with your back to the others, not with your front. Look, I'll show you!"

She climbed over the gate and jumped down into the field. She ran to the surprised brownies. She took hold of one of them and bent him down. He stood up again angrily.

"How dare you push me about!" he cried, in a voice like a thrush's, clear and high. "Go away, you interfering little girl!"

"But I'm only trying to show you how to play leapfrog properly!" said Ina crossly. "Bend down!"

She tried to bend the brownie over again, but he pushed her away and slapped her fingers.

"We play leapfrog the brownie way, not *your* way!" he said. "Brothers, who is this bad-mannered child?"

One of the brownies looked closely at Ina. Then he laughed. "I've heard of her!" he said. "It's Interfering Ina! She pokes her silly little nose into everything and makes herself such a nuisance!"

"Oh, she does, does she?" said the first brownie, glaring at Ina. "Well, every time she interferes in future and pokes her nose into other people's business her nose will get longer! Ha ha! That will be funny!"

He jumped high into the air, turned head over heels, and sprang right over the hedge. The others followed, and Ina was left alone in the field, a little frightened and very cross.

She went home. "Silly little fellows!" she said, feeling her pretty little nose. "As if anything they said would come true!"

She had her dinner, and then she went out to play in the garden. She heard the little boy next door talking to his rabbit as he cleaned out its hutch.

Ina stood on a box and looked over the wall. "Jimmy," she said, "you shouldn't clean out a hutch that way. You should have the clean hay ready before you take out the old hay. You should . . ."

Jimmy stared up at her—and then he stared again. Something funny had happened to Ina's nice little nose. It had grown quite an inch longer.

"What have you done to your nose, Ina?" asked Jimmy in surprise. "It does look funny!"

Ina felt her nose in alarm. Gracious! It did feel long! She rushed indoors and looked at herself in the glass. Yes—it had grown a whole inch longer, and her face looked queer with such a long nose. Ina was ashamed and frightened.

Jimmy stared up at her. Something funny had happened to Ina's nice little nose.

"I shall have to say I bumped it and it swelled," said the little girl to herself. She did not usually tell stories, but she felt too ashamed to say that it had grown long because she had interfered.

So when she went to school that afternoon and the other children asked her what had happened to her nose she told them a story. "I bumped it and it swelled," she said.

"Funny sort of swelling," said John. "It isn't really big—it's just *long*."

Ina forgot about her nose after a bit, for there came a handwork lesson, which she loved. The children were making toys. Ina looked at the little boy next to her.

"What are you making?" she said.

"I'm making an engine," he said.

"That's not the way to make an engine!" said Ina scornfully. "Give it to me. Look—you should put the funnel *here*!" She pressed so hard on the funnel that it broke!

"Oh, you interferer!" said the little boy, almost in tears, for he had been very proud of his engine. "Oooooh! What's happened to your nose, Ina?"

What indeed! It had grown quite two inches longer in that moment, and now it looked horrid! Ina was quite ugly.

The children shouted with laughter.

"Oh, you interferer!" said the little boy almost in tears. "Oooooh!
What's happened to your nose, Ina?"

"Ina's nose is getting longer and longer so that she can poke it into other people's business very easily!" said Joan.

Well, before the day was ended Ina's nose was six inches long. Imagine it! It stuck out from her face and made her look very strange indeed. Her mother was simply horrified when she saw it.

"Ina! What have you done with your nose?"

"Nothing," said Ina sulkily. It was no use saying that she had bumped it, because Mummy simply wouldn't believe her.

"But something's happened to it, something horrid!" said her mother. "I must take you to the doctor."

So Ina went to the doctor, and first he laughed when he saw her nose.

So Ina went to the doctor, and first he laughed when he saw her nose, and then he looked grave, and last of all he looked puzzled.

"I've never seen such a nose," he said. "How did she get it?"

"She won't tell me," said Ina's mother. Then Ina began to cry and she told all that had happened—how she had interfered with the brownies and they had said her nose would grow bigger every time she stuck it into somebody else's business!

"Dear me!" said the doctor in surprise. "So that's what happened. Well, I'm afraid I can't do anything about it."

"But can't you tell us how to cure her nose?" asked Ina's mother, beginning to cry too. "She was such a pretty girl, and now she is so ugly."

"Well, I can only say that perhaps if she stops interfering with other people her nose may go back to its right size," said the doctor. "But that rests with Ina herself, poor child!"

They went home, the mother very sad and upset. So was poor Ina.

In a week's time her nose was almost the right size again, and soon it will be the same pretty little nose she had before.

"Now listen, Ina," said her mother. "We can't have your nose growing any longer, can we? Well, you must stop poking it into things that don't concern you. You mustn't interfere any more. You had better ask the other children to help you."

"All right, Mummy, I will," said Ina. And she went out to find her friends. She told them what the doctor had said.

"So please will you all help me?" she begged. "If I come and interfere, stop me at once, because if you don't my nose will grow down to my toes, and maybe I'll have to tie a knot in it to stop myself from tripping over it!"

"We'll help you, Ina," said the children kindly. Children are always kind when they see someone in trouble, and these children couldn't bear to see Ina crying tears all down her long nose. They had often been cross with her, but now they only wanted to help her.

So the next few days you should have seen what happened. Every time Ina came to interfere or to poke her nose into something that was nothing to do with her they spoke at once. "Ina! Remember! Don't interfere!"

Then Ina would go red and say, "Sorry! I nearly forgot!"

In a week's time her nose was almost the right size again, and soon it will be the same pretty little nose she had before.

But goodness knows how long the magic will last! She will have to be careful all her life not to interfere just in *case* her nose shoots out again! Poor Ina! She still looks a bit queer, but I hope that next time I see her she will look her old pretty little self.

188